# HER HIGHLAND DESTINY

MADELINE MARTIN

*All rights reserved.*

No part of this publication may be sold, copied, distributed, reproduced or transmitted in any form or by any means, mechanical or digital, including photocopying and recording or by any information storage and retrieval system without the prior written permission of both the publisher, Oliver Heber Books and the author, Madeline Martin, except in the case of brief quotations embodied in critical articles and reviews.

PUBLISHER'S NOTE: This is a work of fiction. Names, characters, places, and incidents either are the product of the author's imagination or are used fictitiously. Any resemblance to actual persons, living or dead, business establishments, events, or locales is entirely coincidental.

Copyright Madeline Martin

Published by Oliver-Heber Books

0 9 8 7 6 5 4 3 2 1

# PROLOGUE
## DURHAM, ENGLAND, OCTOBER 1086

It always rained when a child of the Beaumont bloodline was delivered. And certainly the birth of Cassandra Thomas, daughter of Sir Edmund, was no different. Lightning flashed outside and rain lashed against the shutters. Above the roar of the storm came the lusty, indignant cry of Cassandra, perhaps the most special youngest daughter in a line of gifted youngest daughters.

The Beaumont line contained power, granted only to the last born daughters of each generation. Cassandra's mother swept a hand over the babe's face, immediately soothing the child with her ability to manipulate emotions, and handed her to her own mother who could read one's future.

Cassandra gazed up at her eldmother with large, pale blue eyes, silently curious as if pondering her own fate.

"She will be your final daughter borne," her eldmother said with a tender smile at the newest member of her family, the most special of all her grandchildren. "There is great enchantment within her. She will have a connection to the earth, a skill unlike any we've ever seen, and it will give her incredible strength." She paused.

"What is it?" Cassandra's mother asked.

The eldmother gently lay Cassandra on the bed and removed her swaddling. A whisper of a mark glimmered over the infant's right hip, under the tight curl of her leg against her pink body.

"There is more," the older woman said in a whisper of wonder. "She will be chosen as a Protector which also carries its own gifts." Her eldmother's brow furrowed. "Strength - great strength, especially when her force as a Protector is combined with her blessings as a daughter of the Beaumont bloodline."

"When?" Cassandra's mother sat forward with anticipation, alight with joy to have a child of such importance. "When will this greatness happen?"

The eldmother shook her head with a frown. "It is strange, there is a fog preventing me from reading precisely."

Cassandra's mother settled back into a pile of soft pillows and surveyed the sparse room. "It matters not, surely her abilities will manifest themselves with haste and we shall soon witness their extent for ourselves. After all, how long could they possibly take?"

# CHAPTER 1
DURHAM, ENGLAND, OCTOBER 1106

Cassandra could not meet the gaze of her family. Her heart flinched at what she would find there — disappointment. It was like this every year on her birthday, the time when most of the Beaumont women came into their powers. The weeks leading up to the annual mark of her birth brought on a frenzy of excitement and anticipation, and the days afterward crashing into the solemn realization that nothing had happened. Again. For over two decades.

She curled tighter into herself where she hugged the tree branch, hoping no one would search the orchard for her. Year after year, she faced this insurmountable expectation. She hated it. She hated it. She *hated* it.

She yanked an apple off a nearby branch and hurtled it out of the tree where it thunked hollowly into something below.

"Och!"

She jerked upright. Dear Lord, she'd hit someone!

Her own feelings of self-pity were shoved aside and she climbed down the tree to discover what hapless soul might have been felled by her inadvertent blow. Her eldest brother, Phillip was on his knees in the grass, cradling the side of his head. Of course it had been him who had come to speak her. He'd always been the only one who had cared about her more than a legacy. To him, she was a younger sister, a person with her own wishes and dreams.

He lifted his hand from his head, revealing a fat red bump. "I should have known it was you based on that hit. No woman can throw like you. Or man for that matter." Quick as lightning, he snatched an apple from the ground and sent it flying in her direction.

She spun out of its way and hefted a fallen apple, this time intentionally tossing it at him and with less force. It landed on his shoulder and sent spatters of juice flying in all directions.

He cried out dramatically and stuck out his tongue. "It was juicy." He grimaced with great exaggeration, looking more like a cat who'd sucked a lemon rather than her regal brother. "Have a care with the soft ones or mother will have my hide."

"She wouldn't dare skin you, Sir Knight." Cassandra curtseyed sweetly to her brother.

He lowered his head and pounced on her, knocking her to the soft grass where several fallen apples jabbed at her back. She shrieked a laugh and shoved at him. He didn't move, the cur. Very well. She'd play by his game. She grasped his right arm and twisted, careful to avoid breaking the bone. He flinched and Cassandra took advantage of the opportunity to duck free of his weight.

"That only took seconds." He grinned up at her. "You're getting faster."

His words reminded her of why he'd spent hours training her, why he felt she needed protection, why she was out in the orchard in the first place.

"What's the point?" She knew she was being sullen, but couldn't stop the words any more than she could quell the resentment.

He hopped up, his expression serious. "Because someday it might happen. And that's a solid reason for me to ensure you can protect yourself."

She opened her mouth to protest, but he cut her off. "Aye, you're strong, but that isn't enough. You need skill, to be able to defend yourself, and even attack, if necessary." His voice lowered. "The path of a Protector cannot be an easy one."

Protector.

He'd said the word. He actually said it.

Cassandra wanted to block her ears from the word, to cut it from her heart or soul or wherever the foulness of it had attached itself to her. But even if she could somehow remove her eldmother's damning prediction, Cassandra would remain trapped by the expectation of a legacy. She was, after all, still the youngest daughter from a string of youngest daughters in the Beaumont bloodline. After years of watching her mother's belly swell to only reveal two more boys and never grow with child again, Cassandra was indeed the last daughter — the youngest — the one whose blood had been imbued with great powers.

Phillip settled on the ground and patted the spot beside him when she didn't join him.

"I don't want this gift," Cassandra said softly.

"I know." He patted the grass once more. "What makes you the most frightened about it?"

She lowered herself to where he'd indicated. He always had a blunt way of saying things that made her look deep into her heart, beyond the gloss of her emotions. She stared at the distant trees, past the orchard and into herself for the answer.

"I'm afraid I'll fail." The confession came out of her mouth so abruptly and accurately, their impact warmed her eyes and nose.

God's bones, was she about to cry? She looked at the scuffed toes of her kidskin shoes rather than at her brother.

"That is daunting." Phillip shifted. He rolled several apples across the green grass, inspecting each carefully. "I hope you don't presume you're not strong enough or skilled enough. I think we've handled that." He glanced back and winked at her.

"What if I'm not the Protector?" She gasped out a breath. There. She'd said it. Her greatest fear. "What if I'm just a normal woman who is destined to live an ordinary life?"

He lifted an apple from the earth and swept the fruit against his shirt until the golden skin gleamed. "That would imply our soothsayer eldmother was wrong, the bloodline of our ancestors doesn't exist and the humming you feel on the ground is..." He lifted his brows in silent question and bit into the apple.

She smiled softly to herself and spread her hands, palm out, toward the tender green shoots of grass. Sunlight from the copse of trees over her head dappled the skin on the back of her hands with spatters of light. Over the years, the steady vibration of the earth's life had become as silent to her as her own heartbeat. She had to concentrate on the sensation now to even acknowledge it.

Phillip waved the half-eaten apple at her. "Go on."

She closed her eyes and inhaled, tasting the sweet apples scenting the air, letting the sun's heat warm her skin and hair, skimming her palms against the cool grass. Her hands hovered and she fixed on the steady drone buried deep in the rich, black soil. It started like a low buzz at first, the way a lazy bee might sound as it languidly flew through a field of summer flowers, then it whirred in a chorus of energy, rising around her, singing to her the beauty of its being. But there was something else. Something deeper.

Perspiration prickled along her brow, but she ignored it and forced her attention on the tenuous connection between her soul and that of the earth. A high-pitched ring echoed in the distance. Not a ring — a cry. Mourning. The hollowness of misery rose over the din of life until it filled Cassandra's ears and mind and heart. Sorrow spread through her like shadows and swept off in rolling waves. So much sadness.

Strong hands caught her shoulders and shook her. The connection severed and she was snapped back, away from her awareness.

"What is it, Cassandra?" Phillip's ashen face was mere inches from her own, his apple lay discarded and forgotten on the ground. "Why are you crying?"

She brought her hands to her face and found them trembling uncontrollably. She brushed her fingertips over her cheeks and they came away damp with her tears.

The deafening cries of the earth had fallen to a whisper with her broken connection. Phillip put his face in front of hers, his blue eyes locked on her. "Look at me, Cass. Look. At. Me." He bit the words out, his tone so stark, it drew her from the horror.

"Breathe," he commanded.

She obeyed. Air rushed into her body and the tension gripping her eased until finally her breath came on its own accord rather than by order.

His brow relaxed, if only slightly. "What is it, Cassandra? What have you seen?"

She suppressed the urge to give in to the threat of her tears once more. "The earth is crying."

"What does that mean?" Fear rendered his pupils to specks of black in his pale blue eyes and sent a jab of ice to her heart.

She shook her head. "I don't know."

"Is it time?" His hands on her shoulders gripped tighter, as if he meant to keep her locked there forever.

"I don't know."

He nodded. "Come, you should be inside."

Cassandra glared at the house. If it was time, she wanted her family to be no part of it. She didn't want their cajoling and honeyed platitudes sending her on her way. "Don't tell them."

He stared down at her for a long pause. His face smoothed for the first time since the awful conversation. "Of course." His expression turned playful and he offered her a deep, groveling bow. "I am eternally at your service, my lady."

She ruffled his dark curls, so like her own, but shorn close to his head to give him an advantage in battle. "I'll hold you to your word to keep mum about telling the rest." Despite her attempt to continue the lighter tone, her voice came out flat and Phillip's mood sobered.

He rose and nodded.

They parted ways at the house as nonchalantly as possible with Phillip striding toward the solar and Cassandra climbing the polished wood staircase to the long hall. A sudden warmth spread over the right side of her hip, like a breath fanning over her skin. A gasp choked from her and she drew back, away from...from nothing. She clasped her hands against the warm spot and looked at the fabric there. Naught showed against the pale pink linen. Its smooth surface lay cool and unassuming against her body, as if the sensation had never happened.

Strange.

She ran to her room on shaking legs and her hands slipped over the latch in her haste. She needed to be alone, to breathe, to relive that moment in the orchard when she experienced the power of the earth weeping even as she wanted desperately to forget it. Her mind swam so fast, it felt as though bits of it were flying loose.

What was happening to her?

Finally she burst through the door and secured it behind her. She grasped the heavy, voluminous skirt of her cote in her fists and yanked it up, over her legs and up past her hip. A mark showed upon her skin where the warmth had flared. It was in the shape of a dagger with the point tilted down to her left foot, mottled brown as though it were simply a birth mark.

But what was the meaning of it?

She stroked a hand over it. The mark was not raised or indented. Nay, it was flush as if it had always been part of her skin.

An image flashed in her mind. Green and blue waters, fed from a nearby waterfall. Grass hugged against every side. The apparition was so close to her, the damp cool air kissed at her skin. A sparkle glinted in the shallows of the colorful water. A green gem? She stepped closer and her feet shuffled under the soft grass underfoot. She dropped the hem of her cote and stretched her hand to the water, reaching, reaching. Her fingers dipped into the icy pool. The vision rippled and disappeared.

Cassandra cried out in disappointment and stared down at her outstretched hands where evidence of having touched water glistened in a slant of sunlight streaming in from the open shutters. Wherever that was, she needed to find its location.

Now.

"Lady Cassandra?" a quiet, feminine voice said. The maid who had been both companion and servant to Cassandra in their twenty years growing up together stood in the doorway.

"I fear I must leave at once, Mary. Please, be so kind as to fetch Phillip." Cassandra looked out to the long road winding from their small manor. The trail pulled at her, beckoning with urgency. "And tell no one else of my departure."

∽

EDINBURGH, Scotland

The seventh knight staggered back and scrambled to kneel in resignation before Fergus the Undefeated. The conquered knight leaned heavily against his blade, and gasped to reclaim the breath knocked from him. Rain pattered down on their chain mail, leaving the padded clothing beneath soaked through to the skin. The squires would be required to apply a solid rubbing of oil to the chain that evening.

Six others had come before the newly fallen man, and each had clamored with as much haste to draw the line of surrender in their battle. Fergus had purposefully made sure never to hurt another of his fellow knights at practice, but apparently his efforts had not subdued their fears.

He clasped the man's lifted hand and aided him to his feet. "Ye did well." Fergus clapped him on the back and instantly regretted it when the man winced.

"Sir Fergus." A young man with tousled blonde hair stood bravely in front of him. His chain mail was new enough to reflect the gray sky with a gleam like freshly wrought silver. "I would be honored to fight ye, The Undefeated."

"Ye may want to try when yer armor shows the effects of war a bit." Fergus made to flank the young knight, but the lad cut in front of him once more.

The young man set his chin stubbornly. "I've been watching ye for years and now I can finally have my chance."

"For years?" Fergus chuckled, flattered despite himself. Who was he to stop a lad from his dream? "Ready yerself."

The young man's eyes went wide in his face with eagerness. He shoved his head into the equally new helm and held his sword. Fergus huffed out an exhale and concentrated on his opponent the way he always did during battle, utilizing his gift.

He shoved through the emotions and thoughts and fears emanating from his foes; those were merely distractions. Nay, he wanted the movement of energy around them, the tick that would betray the move they thought before their body had time to execute.

Likewise, Fergus directed a fraction of his attention on

himself, to absorb the force his body created with each move, masking them completely from even the most astute of opponents.

The lad's intended movements radiated from his left arm. Fergus blocked the hit before the young knight could attempt the strike.

The wind shifted and carried with it a sweet, familiar fragrance. Apples. Fergus' nostrils flared at the aroma. There were no orchards nearby, at least none he'd noticed, and it was nearly too late for apple season. A hum crackled in the air and brought on a wet, earthy scent, like rain. Fergus' hair stood on end.

Magic.

His heart slammed with a frenzy in his chest. The presence of it hissed everywhere, reminding him of that night.

*Nay.*

He wanted to clutch his head in his hands and roar until his throat bled, he wanted to claw at his chest until his heart was a pathetic pulsing bloody pulp in his palms. He would endure any injury over the memories of *that* night.

Fergus jerked to the side, as though doing so would wrench the memory free and fling it from his mind. But it was not that night that came to him. The rain parted and peeled away the gray sky for sunlight to pour in. Fergus squinted against the brilliance, but did not pull away his gaze.

A woman's face appeared at its center, one he'd never seen before. She was young, her skin practically white against the dark mass of curls spilling over her shoulders. Her gaze flicked up and met his, a piercing blue. A flush of pink showed on her cheeks and lips, giving her the allure of true innocence. Confusion crossed her comely features. Her hand moved over her right hip, the opposite side as his mark, but in the same place, and he knew.

The stone had passed to its new Protector.

A dulled practice sword thwacked against his chest, but he did not move.

The former Protector was dead. She'd hidden herself away for well over a decade, impossible to find despite Fergus' efforts to find her. He'd searched with desperation, all to no avail. There was a new Protector now, which meant he would have another opportunity to lure her back to King Edgar, and there would be another opportunity to claim the stone as his.

His mind spun with possibilities and what they might bring to him. After years of fruitless searching, and as many years of separation from the son he had never met, he may finally have his opportunity.

The practice sword skimmed off the shoulder of his chain mail. Fergus had completely forgotten their mock battle. He turned his head to regard the youth, and the young man stepped back. Rightly so.

Power thrummed through Fergus' veins with all the force of a decade of rage and loss and longing. A single blow could kill the lad.

"We're done," Fergus said flatly.

The lad nodded. "Mayhap again? At another time?" He watched Fergus with a hopeful expression.

"There is business requiring my attention."

The young man gave a slight bow. "It was an honor to fight with ye."

Fergus inclined his head respectfully and quit the training yard for the palace. Inside, King Edgar sat on his throne as he did most days, his elbows rested against the carved sides of the regal seat, his fingers steepled between them. He flicked a hand outward in dismissal of others.

"Leave us," King Edgar's voice echoed in the large stone room.

Advisors and petitioners alike silently obeyed the order, streaming past Fergus' large frame in a clatter of footsteps on the stone floor. The last man out pulled the massive doors shut behind him, letting them close with a deafening slam. Silence followed while the king stared down at Fergus.

There was an arrogant victory about the king, not outwardly, but a glow deep inside his chest where the rest of him was rotten and dark. He already knew.

"The Protector is dead." Fergus spoke as if he was unaware of the king's knowledge. Likewise, he concentrated on keeping his own emotions and thoughts contained within himself.

He was not certain how the king came upon his uncanny revelations, whether he himself had power, or someone else in his employ did, but Fergus knew better than to let his own thoughts be read and heard.

King Edgar's eyes widened. "I am aware. Which means a new Protector will have been found. I'm assuming ye can find this one."

Fergus gave a sharp nod.

The king's fingers separated from where they steepled together and clawed over the arms of his throne like long limbed insects. "I was too lenient last time. I see as much now."

Fergus said nothing, focusing instead on muffling the rapid beat of his heart and silencing his racing thoughts.

"Find the stone this time and bring the lass here." The king paused to lift a gilded chalice from a tray beside his throne. He drank long and deep so the lump in the middle of his long, skinny neck bobbed several times before he set the cup aside. Moisture clung to his upper lip, but he did not blot it away. "Ye have two moon cycles to bring them both to me."

"If I do not?" Fergus pressed.

"There will be consequences." King Edgar's mouth curled up in a wolfish grin. "Consequences ye willna like."

Fergus did not respond. Why bother when he had no choice?

The king swept the back of his hand toward Fergus, dismissing him as one might wave away an annoying fly.

Fergus put his back to the king and walked the long stretch of flagstone leading to the door. His feet echoed off the cold stone walls. He used the sound to keep himself in the moment, to lock his concentration to hold his thoughts to himself.

"Do not let me down, Fergus the Undefeated." The title was said with a drawn out taunt.

The Undefeated. How Fergus hated the name, the intentional mockery King Edgar had bestowed while knighting him after that damned night. For truly there was no man as defeated in all the land as he.

## CHAPTER 2

The call of the stone was stronger on Skye, pulling Cassandra beyond the desire for sleep or food. Her bones ached from the constant sway of the saddle and hunger gnawed at her belly. It had been well over a fortnight since she'd left her home in Durham, perhaps longer. Some of her travel had been ridden on the back of her horse, some thicker areas walked through by foot, and still others requiring a vessel to carry her over water.

The skies rained down upon her for the better part of a week. She was drenched and her hands were locked in clawed fists from her grip on the reins. Though it was not yet winter, the cold froze her breath and her constant shivering left her back and ribs aching.

She had not known what to expect in being the Protector, but it was certainly not this.

Her upper body lay against the horse's neck, seeking whatever heat she might gain from it. The beast trudged along, heedless of her suffering.

Cassandra blinked her heavy eyes once, twice. The third time they remained closed and a peaceful warmth spread through her, as though she were back home in the sunlit meadow of the orchard. She tried to push that memory from her mind, for it was too painful to recall – a time when she had been warm and well fed, when expectation was the worst of her worries.

Only it was not the orchard which blossomed in her thoughts, but a terrain very much like what she traveled in presently along with a man.

His chain mail initially made her assume the knight might be Phillip. But nay, Phillip had a brown steed and this man rode one as black as night. The man's dark hair was longer than Phillip's, coming down to his shoulders rather than cropped neat and close. Hoofbeats echoed in her head, growing louder, faster. Closer.

His expression was ferocious where it fixed on the path before him, his jaw locked with steely determination. He straightened and turned his head toward her, his gaze so dark his eyes appeared to be black. Their stares locked and she knew he could see her from wherever he was, as clearly as she saw him.

She drew a sharp inhale and sat upright on her steed, no longer weary. The image cleared away as though it'd never been there, much as the waters with the glittering gem had done when she'd first gotten the mark. And like the gem, she knew the man to be real.

An urgency filled her, stronger than before, pulling her, driving her to make haste to the fairy pools. The horse rode onward on powerful legs as though drawn with the same level of intensity as she. The wind roared, and the landscape flashed by with incredible speed.

All at once, her horse stopped and nearly sent her flying over its neck. Mist hung in the air like a gauzy curtain, blocking their path. Cassandra rocked in the saddle and clicked her tongue.

The horse did not move. She looked behind her where there had been no haze, and once more to the front where it blanketed the trail.

The horse stamped its hoof to the ground. Restless, the beast shifted, only to stop and rear back.

Clearly it would not go any further. Perhaps it could not. Cassandra patted its neck and leapt to the ground. She drew her pole arm from the saddle. If nothing else, she would not be unarmed. Not with images of the knight still pounding through her mind.

She drew a deep breath and plunged into the fog. The air within was dewy and cool and thick enough, she could scarce see two paces in front of her. She clung to her pole arm and tapped it along the ground in an effort to avoid any large objects which might impede her path.

Water trickled in the distance. Her heart pounded and her blood roared through her veins. She was close. So close.

The wall of vapor cleared away and opened to a sunlit mountainside. Emerald grass shone in the golden light and large pools of blue-green water sparkled under wide-open skies. Her racing heart slammed to a stop.

She knew this place.

The gem had been there. She surveyed frantically over the surface of the clear water to the shallow depths beneath. No stone glinted back at her. She glanced up the sloping face of the mountain and found a number of such pools, all linked together with trickling streams and waterfalls. One of them must contain the stone.

She strode up the steep side to the next bit of water and glanced about the shimmering surface. Something flew past her peripheral on the opposite side of the multi-colored pools, silent and unexpected. A man.

He raced up the side of the mountain as though his life

depended upon it. She straightened in shock. His movements had been too fast, too soundless.

Without hesitation, she ran after him, following on her side of the water. Clearly he knew where the stone was, given his haste, and it was not where she had wasted time searching.

His dark gaze met hers and her step faltered. It was him. The man she had seen only moments ago in her mind.

He stopped as well and stared, his powerful chest rising and falling beneath his chain mail with rapid breath. Lines creased the skin between his heavy, dark brows, as though he were concentrating. He was larger in person than in her vision. Much larger. He could crush her if she were a normal woman. Was this man someone she ought to defeat?

They stared at one another for the span of a long heartbeat before the urgency shrieked at her, spurring her onward once more.

He darted forward the exact moment she did, as though their bodies were connected. That's when it caught her eye. The glimmer of a sparkle in the depths of a pool between them.

The stone.

Cassandra charged into the thigh deep water. Its chill hit her like a punch, but she pressed onward, dragging her heavy skirts behind her. Her legs burned with the effort, yet still she moved too slowly. The man roared with each step, for surely his chain mail dragged him back as much as her skirts did her. Together they raced with torturous slowness.

Her heart threatened to leap out of her chest. This was her destiny. She could not fail.

The rock beneath her foot shifted and slipped out from under her, sending her sprawling face first into the water. As she fell, the man lunged and thrust his hand into the water where the gem sparkled.

She floundered in the pool in an attempt to find purchase on the slick ground beneath her. Finally her feet caught and she launched herself to standing once more. He might have claimed the stone, but she would not fail.

∼

Fergus groped blindly in the water, skimming over the rocky floor in an attempt to claim the gem. Finally he caught at a chain and the stone pulled safely into the cradle of his palm. Energy seared through him. Hot. Bright. Powerful.

Too powerful.

His bones shuddered and his skin burned. Pain seared through his gut and spiraled outward as though the force of it intended to tear him apart. Everything in him screamed for him to let go. But he did not. He had too much to lose to fail now.

Nay, he clasped his other hand over his fist, securing the stone lest it wrench free.

His blood heated in his veins, igniting with raw strength.

*She was worried about him.*

The thought carried in on the overwhelming surge and settled him back into the quiet path of pools trickling down the mountainside. He opened his eyes to find the woman standing a pace away from him, the determination on her face softened by the glow of concern in her eyes.

What had once been a lightly pulsing sense of awareness had taken on a more poignant quality. He could not only assume her thoughts, he could practically hear them.

*She thought the stone was hers, and intended to get it back.*

Nay, he could actually hear them.

*She meant to get it back by any means necessary.*

Fergus removed one hand from the stone and pulled free his sword. It hissed menacingly from the scabbard. It was meant to intimidate, but she did not back down.

His chest tightened. He did not wish to battle this young woman. Her body was slender within her cote, her arms impossibly skinny in the tapered sleeves, like sticks he might snap. And yet defiance shone in her pale blue eyes and her sharp chin set in a stubborn glower.

*She would not go down without a fight.*

Damn it, he didn't want her to go down at all.

"I dinna want to fight ye, lass." He stepped back and slipped the stone's simple gold chain around his neck. The heat of it warmed through his chain mail, the padded shirt beneath, the linen under that and to the skin of his chest.

Instead of answering, her energy arced out toward him in preparation to attempt a hit. He stepped to the side, and her energy shifted to follow him. The move was immediate and without hesitation. Too fast.

Never had an opponent moved so quickly before. This baffled him and cost him a fraction of a second before he could think to move again.

Her pole arm slammed into his chest hard enough to tear the breath from his lungs. He gasped for a drag of cool air and his chest ached with the effort.

What the hell? How did that scrap of a lass get a hit like that on a man his size?

The lines of her energy drew back again and this time he treated her preparation with more consideration. He lifted his sword to block the blow as the pole arm came down on him.

How did she move so bloody fast?

Her heel slammed into the back of his knees, catching him off guard. The hit rocked his balance and sent him careening backward into the pool. She was on him, her arms coiled around his, her legs entwined with his, a viper of death intent on drowning him. Her fingers patted over his chest, seeking the stone.

*The stone. The stone. The stone.*
*Her destiny.*

He grasped the back of her dress and ripped her from his body. She flew off him, arms and legs outstretched in a fruitless attempt to cling onto him. The woman fought like a damn harpy.

He dragged himself to his feet, sending water flooding off him and dripping from the tightly linked chain mail he wore. The armor weighed practically more than he did. It was a wonder she hadn't succeeded in drowning him.

She lay face down in the water, unmoving.

Shite.

He stared at her, but saw no ripples in her energy. She'd die if he left her as she lay. If she did, a new Protector would be chosen, and who knew where he'd find the next one.

He heaved a sigh, waded to her still form, and dragged her from the water. She weighed next to nothing, even with her clothing and hair sodden. A sputtering sound gurgled from her chest. He tilted her above the water, and she gave a savage choking cough that expelled the liquid from her lungs.

*Cold. She was cold. Freezing.*

Jesu, her discomfort was so intense, an icy chill settled into the depths of Fergus' very bones and cooled him as well. He set her on the sunlit grass and felt the heat of it seep into her back as surely as though it were him lying there.

Her eyes remained closed, her lashes a dark sweep against pale cheeks. He stared down at her for a long moment, transfixed by her beauty. Again.

The last time had almost cost him the stone. But then, she'd been so lovely when she'd stumbled after catching sight of him. As though she had been as taken aback.

Those beautiful blue eyes had focused on him and his world had fallen away. Those luscious black curls now lay in thick, wet waves, but he could all too easily recall how they shone glossy about her fair face. Despite being so very cold and still, her lips were brilliant red and stood out like rose petals against her porcelain skin.

Had he not experienced the hit she'd delivered him, he would have thought her the most delicately beautiful thing in all the world. He stroked a hand down her smooth cheek and her breath drew in, swelling her bosom upward.

*She liked his touch. She found it warm. Comforting.*

He snatched his hand back. He had no right to touch her. She was his enemy.

It was that final thought which brought him to his senses and reminded him of his obligation. He could not waste any more time, not when he knew the price of his delay.

A feminine whisper sounded on the wind, distant and impossible to decipher. His hair prickled and a chill shivered over his skin.

He narrowed his gaze and surveyed the surrounding area. The sound intensified, a chant of lyrical vowels and hard consonants echoing in his mind. It filled his head until it crushed against his brain and threatened to crack open his skull.

He clutched his head in his hands and grunted through the agony. The pain did not abate. He tossed his head from side to side, but the scent of magic was everywhere. Foul and inescapable.

*Leave.*

The word resonated through his suffering. He backed away and the hurt ebbed. He staggered back further and the torturous grip eased from his temples.

A figure stood in the distance, her body masked in a green hooded cloak. She lifted a hand, the action so smooth, it didn't generate any pre-movement energy, as though she knew how to absorb her actions before moving the way he did.

Magic crackled in the air and left a heavy scent of moisture, redolent of the moments before a torrential storm. Lightning streaked across the sky, yet the rain did not come. His skin hummed with the power flickering and snapping around him. Such incredible energy. So much. If he could harness it, learn to use it, he would be unstoppable.

"*Neathu*," she whispered.

A blanket of milky fog rolled in front of him, draping his view of the Protector and the witch.

Fear grappled Fergus momentarily. The Protector was lost to him. He needed her. Damn it. He needed her.

*The witch had spent almost all her energy on him. A few more moments would have killed her.*

Even her thoughts in his mind were faint with exhaustion. If he had withstood the affliction of her curse a bit longer, he would have won.

As it was, he had not truly lost.

He curled his fingers against the stone. He had it, and the Protector would try to get it back. Rather than stumble blind through the mist, he would bide his time. She would find him, and when she did - he would convince her to join him.

He would have the stone and the Protector, exactly as was deemed necessary by the king. Then, at long last, Fergus would have his son.

## CHAPTER 3

Cassandra startled awake and grasped at empty air. There was no stone. No pools. No man. Firelight flickered off natural stone walls and the roar of swiftly falling water came from somewhere very nearby. The sweet scent of burning sage hovered above the musty odor of a cave long left damp.

The small pallet she lay upon, however, as well as the simple table and chairs by a lit fire, indicated someone resided in the cave. The man?

"Ye're awake." A woman's voice spoke gently and echoed within the enclosed space. She straightened from where she'd crouched before the fire and drew back her green hood to reveal thick raven locks and a strong chin. Her eyes were pale, though it was difficult to discern their color in the gilded light of the fire.

A sense of peace exuded from the dark haired woman and although Cassandra did not know who the stranger was, she had no fear.

The woman smiled kindly. "Welcome to Skye, Protector."

"A terrible Protector I've turned out to be," Cassandra said miserably.

The woman blinked at Cassandra. "Ye're English?"

"Aye."

"I dinna expect the Protector to be English." The woman's soft laugh was without malice.

"You are sure you have the correct woman?" Cassandra asked, unable to stem the tide of hope rising in her. None of this had been as she expected. After a lifetime of preparing for this moment, surely she could not have already failed.

"Do ye bear the sign of a dagger on yer right hip?"

Cassandra nodded.

"Then aye, ye're the keeper of the Heart of Scotland." The woman's expression sobered. "The former Protector died days ago and the transfer of the mark would have happened then."

Cassandra put her hand to the symbol on her hip, so recently emblazoned on her skin, she could still recall the strange wash of heat. "How do you come by such knowledge?"

"I am a priestess of the stone." She inclined her head. "I am called Morag and have been given information passed down through the centuries to bestow upon ye."

Cassandra's shoulders relaxed somewhat. Having someone to guide her on her quest would make it easier, would it not? Countless questions buzzed through her mind and came to rest on the large man with dark eyes who had been at the pool. The way he'd looked at her, as though he were mesmerized by her. It was too easy to bring to mind again and again. In fact, it did so without her meaning to.

But, nay, she would not ask about him. Not yet. "Has the stone been in the water for centuries?" she asked finally.

"When a Protector dies with the stone in their possession, the stone returns here to the mystical fairy pools and waits to be claimed."

"I didn't claim it." Cassandra shifted her gaze from Morag to the crude table. A massive chunk of cheese rested on the wooden surface along with a loaf of bread. Despite the pang of

Cassandra's regret at having failed to get the stone, hunger rasped within her belly.

"It isna always so." Morag approached the table, lifted a slender knife and sliced a thick wedge of cheese. She handed both the cheese and loaf of bread to Cassandra.

The bread was warm against her palm, and crusty, as though it'd been not long out of the oven. Her mouth watered with urgency. Instead she swallowed and shook her head. "I cannot take your food."

Morag was already walking away. "Eat. Recover yer strength. When ye have gotten the rest and sustenance ye've deprived yerself of, and when ye've learned enough of yer task, then ye may go after the stone. Then ye will be ready."

Cassandra daintily broke a corner of the cheese off to nibble at in a ladylike fashion. No sooner had the creamy, sharp cheese touched her tongue, a ravenous hunger nearly took over. She tried to chew with decorum, but her mouth watered too ferociously.

Morag placed a cup of wine in front of her. Cassandra had not been so thirsty until that very moment, when faced with the prospect of drinking again. Her throat burned for liquid. She lifted it with shaking hands to her lips where she drained the sweet wine in two large gulps. Her mouth had been so very dry, her stomach so empty. It was a wonder she had been able to make it as long as she had on so little.

"The stone enhances one's powers." Morag refilled the cup from a ewer of wine and placed a hunk of dried beef in front of Cassandra. "Everyone has special abilities granted from the stone, and they will grow stronger when it is on their person. Each skill is different, as is each person's experience in getting their mark, claiming the stone, taking guardianship of the stone..." She trailed off with a smile. "I believe you understand."

Cassandra nodded and bit an unladylike chunk from the

bread. The crust flaked apart against her tongue, and her teeth sank into the tender white center. She almost moaned with delight.

"He mustn't be allowed to keep the stone," Morag warned, her tone ominous.

A trickle of icy fear crept up Cassandra's spine. She set aside the cup and stared at the priestess.

"He sought the stone for selfish purposes." Morag set the ewer upon the small table. "His intent is not to ensure the safety and prosperity of Scotland like you. If he is allowed to keep the stone, Scotland will suffer for his avarice. The earth will lose her balance and great storms will plague Scotland with famine and pestilence and death to follow."

"When will this happen?" Cassandra demanded.

"Some will begin immediately, but the worst will follow in two moon cycles."

"I must go now." Cassandra leapt to her feet, but exhaustion caught at her and she stumbled backward.

Morag smiled sadly. "If yer fate is as yer predecessors, ye have a lifetime of battle ahead of ye. The war between light and dark is one driven by the balance of life and will ensue until the end of time. Rest, my dear. Ye may leave in the morning. Then yer fight will begin in earnest."

The man's image filled Cassandra's mind. The impossibly large man with dark eyes and dark hair, the way he'd stopped in his desperate charge to stare at her, as though he were fascinated. Curious, mayhap. Her pulse flickered at her memory. She had not been unaffected. Would she truly need to battle him?

She supposed she would discover as much once she found him, and she knew she would. The earth hummed beneath her feet with an eagerness to lead her to him. She would have to reclaim the stone, even if it did mean a fight. Though in the depths of her heart, she hoped it did not.

THE WOMAN HAD BEGUN to follow Fergus the prior day. He'd sensed her presence as soon as she'd left the veiled cover of the mystical pools. She moved swiftly, and with purpose, and yet even though he was just south of the Isle of Skye, she took long enough to strain his fragile patience.

Fergus paced his narrow room in the inn. It had already seemed small when he'd first rented the chamber, but now its walls threatened to crush in against him with more insistence, its ceiling impossibly low. Anticipation was getting the better of him.

He put his hand over the stone where it lay tucked beneath his leine. Power pulsed against his skin. But it was not anything he would possess forever. Even if he had intended to keep it for his own, he would never grow accustomed to its warm, unnatural glow.

It didn't stink of magic. Not like the witch had. But it was reminiscent of it all the same, filled with too many bitter memories. The sensation of it prickled at his skin. He wanted to scrub his hands over his body and remove every bit of it from his person. If the stone did not heighten his ability to read people, if he did not need it on his person to bring to Edgar in bartering for his son, he would throw the blasted thing away.

For now, it was half of what the king required. Once Fergus had the woman in his possession, he would make haste to Edinburgh where King Edgar awaited the woman and the stone. The idea of it was simple, an exchange of sorts - the stone and the Protector for the boy.

The boy.

Fergus snorted derisively into the empty room. He didn't even know the lad's name. In every way, he had failed as a father. First he'd failed to protect the lad's mother, then when he'd been persuaded by the king to join his guard, he'd accepted in the hopes of finding the lad within the keep somewhere. All attempts to locate his son had met with more failure. The king was a crafty devil.

The sweet scent of apples caressed Fergus' senses and took the edge off the restlessness rattling through him. She was near.

He lifted his pack from the floor and strode from the crude rented room. It would be better for her to assume she caught him rather than discover him awaiting her arrival. His horse whinnied upon his arrival, the massive black hooves stamping into the hay-covered earth in the stable.

Fergus swung into the saddle and urged his steed through the streets, away from the dismal village. The sun shone openly upon him, the sky a stretch of clear, cloudless blue. He rode on for the lesser part of an hour when he sensed her. The force of her energy swelled against him, rendering her presence unmistakable. An eagerness sizzled through his veins and surprised him.

He could too easily recall the flush of her cheeks and mouth, the gentleness of her face. She intrigued and enticed him, a delicate wisp of a thing who hit stronger than any knight he'd ever fought.

Then again, mayhap it had been his surprise at finding she could hit at all. Perchance she was not as strong as he remembered. Soon he would find out, and this time he would pay careful attention.

Only her attack did not come when expected. She hung back, hidden from sight. Indeed, if it wasn't for the wavering warmth of her presence lapping at his awareness, he would have assumed she'd left.

Like a true warrior with proper training, she bided her time, her patience immeasurable. She didn't attack when he'd stopped to camp, nor when he'd hunted his supper, or even when he'd stopped to eat the roasted meat. Nay, it was long after he'd lain still in his bedroll, beyond the time it took before the fire smoldered into glowing red embers. That's when the sweet scent of summer apples filled the cave where he'd taken refuge.

Her movement rippled through his consciousness though her feet made not the slightest shuffle. She crept close enough so he could feel her like a wave of heat. His nostrils flared at her delicious scent, as though he might devour the smell as readily as he could the fruit.

She stood over him, but did not move to attack. He curled his hand around the hilt of his dagger and waited.

Nothing happened. Her breathing remained smooth and even, while her movements did not arc out toward him to indicate her intention of an attack. What the devil was she getting at?

He opened his eyes and stared up at her. She did not flinch from his glare.

God's teeth but she was beautiful. A dark cloak had been pulled over her black curls. It shaded her face and left her eyes glowing pale and luminous in the firelight. She crouched near him, yet her hands were free of a weapon.

"Why do ye no' attack?" he demanded.

"I do not wish to fight," she answered simply. Her voice melted over him like honey, light and feminine, quietly breathy.

"Because ye will fail," he surmised.

"I do not fear defeat. Nor do I fear you." She tilted her head. "I think I may be one of the few who does not."

She was correct, but he would not give voice to such affirmations. Not when he was unsure what she was about. He sensed curiosity from her, but naught else. No malice, nor ill intent.

"I believe you do not wish to fight me." She eased from her crouch into a more comfortable sitting position beside him, her legs crossing beneath the heavy length of her skirt. The wool lay against her calves and outlined the fine curves. "You said as much before. Do you still feel that way?"

This lass made him think little of battle and more of loving. A strange consideration, as he had not been tempted in many, many years. Not since Allisandre. Ten long years ago.

He sat up in his bedroll and assumed a similarly relaxed posture with one arm casually slung over his bent right knee. "I dinna want to fight ye. But I fear it may be unavoidable."

Her eyes settled on him, pale in the firelight. But he'd seen them in the daylight and knew them to be the fairest blue, like an iced loch in the middle of winter and rimmed with a ring of sapphire. They were fringed with lashes as dark as her black curls, and just as thick. Eyes that could steal a man's soul.

"Because you have the stone," she whispered.

"Aye," he answered in a gravelly voice. "Because I have it and I know ye want it."

## CHAPTER 4

Cassandra leaned toward the warrior with the dark mysterious eyes, half crawling to the lure of him. His heartbeat mingled with the earth and thrummed in a sweet, enticing melody. She had sensed it before, she realized, when she'd first seen him.

But, at the time, her heart had been pounding too loud in her ears to discern it in the chaos.

She stared down at his massive chest, where a slight lump rose from beneath his chain mail. The stone. Her body edged forward as though drawn toward him. She lifted her gaze to his penetrating stare.

"Aye," she said in a sultry tone she did not recognize as her own. "I want the stone."

His gaze trailed over her body, bold and unabashed. She ought to have been offended by his impertinence and should have been inclined to deliver a righteous slap upon his cheek. And yet her heart pounded too hard for her to move. Her blood ignited with a delicious heat and her nipples prickled with a sexual consciousness she'd not yet experienced.

"Is that all ye want?" he asked in a thick brogue. His eyes glittered with understanding in the low light.

His brow was creased with a lifetime of worry, but his lips were full and supple beneath his neatly trimmed beard. She found herself watching his mouth, wondering what it might feel like against hers, what he might taste like.

"I think ye'd taste like apples." He leaned on one arm, moving closer. "Crisp and sweet and fresh."

The breath fled her lips and her throat went dry. A virgin's fear within her warred with a woman's curiosity.

"That's what ye smell like." His eyes lowered and she realized he stared at her mouth with the same intensity as she gazed at his.

"Like what?" she breathed.

"Apples." He said it in a growling exhale, the sound intimately primitive.

Except it didn't scare her, it excited her. The blood shot quickly through her veins with heat and an anticipation she did not understand. She wanted to experience it all - the quiet, cool night, the wash of flickering golden light, the heady power of the stone blazing only inches from her hand, and that beautiful mouth set beneath the darkness of his beard.

"I smell like apples." Her lips curled at the thought.

"If ye dinna mean to kill me, why come here?" He shifted nearer still, until he was practically bowing over her.

Cassandra's body thrummed with heat and longing. Should she feel this way about the man with whom she was supposed to be locked in a lifelong battle? It hadn't occurred to her to ask Morag at the time.

But then, she had never expected to feel *this*.

The heat of desire was unmistakable. She stared up at him, not backing down from his question.

"Why are ye here, Protector?" His gaze raked down her body.

She arched her breasts upward, her essence alight with sexuality. With need.

"For the stone," she gasped. "For you."

"For me." He caught her waist in his massive arms and dragged her body against his.

A surprised moan escaped her lips. He could kill her right now, drag a blade across her exposed throat while her core burned with lust. She ought to flee.

The earth pulsed under her, almost undulating, encouraging her toward him. But there was something else. Heat rolled off him, like fire, threatening to consume her with the force of his own desire.

*He wanted her.*

The knowledge of his thoughts rolled in her mind and prickled through her with sharp, tangible awareness.

He ran a powerful hand down her back and clasped her bottom, nudging her hips against his where the heat of his manhood rose hard between them. "This is what ye want?"

Mortification blazed through her. What had she wanted? Not this. It was too much. Too soon. The force of his mind in hers, their shared need welling like fire between them. She had a purpose.

It was not the stone. She needed the stone.

Her teeth sank into her bottom lip and she slid her glance away, her emotions warring. He struggled too, somehow she sensed it.

"Ach, too much then?" He eased back and his touch smoothed over her waist. "Do ye want a lover's touch? Caresses and teasing?"

She trembled. She, who had waited for the honor of her role as Protector, who had learned how to best a man in combat and had trekked countless miles through the rugged Scottish terrain to find the stone, trembled.

The stone.

She needed the stone.

*He wanted her to forget.*

His palm cradled her jaw and he stared deep into her eyes. His pupils melted into the vast darkness of his irises. Beautiful.

She lost herself in the intensity of his stare, of his desire. His thumb swept over her lower lip and freed it from her teeth. He shook his head in chastisement and gently lowered his mouth to hers.

His beard tickled over her chin as his lips touched hers, warm and surprisingly soft. He tasted of the roasted rabbit he'd eaten at dinner and the sweetness of ale. His mouth closed over her lower lip in a delicate, savoring kiss - this man whose name she did not know, who had something she so desperately needed. She ought to be fighting him, not kissing him.

And yet she tilted her head to return the intimate gesture when the tip of his tongue swept against her mouth. She moaned softly and he grew more daring with his kiss, deepening it with his tongue and stoking the fires of her lust.

*He could not stop himself from kissing her, wanting her at his side, and yet he hated himself for it.*

She sensed betrayal lingering in his thoughts, so easily read it was as though he spoke to her.

Yet the lust was as apparent, if not more so. His emotions in her soul, his voice in her mind – all of it served only to heighten her own desire. She put her hands to his chest and found them shifting higher of their own volition, toward that lump beneath his chain mail. To the Heart of Scotland.

He jerked back and eyed her with suspicion. "Leave it."

The connection between them fell away and she no longer could sense what he thought, nor could she feel the presence of his emotions.

"Who do you betray?" she asked.

His fingers ran lightly over the ground and his face reflected a furrow of concentration.

"You hated yourself for kissing me, but you couldn't stop." Cassandra frowned. "You are betraying someone. Are you wed?"

"I was." He put his palm to the ground and studied his hand. "Ye can read thoughts as well?"

As well? He had powers as she did? "Only when you kissed me. I could hear what was in your mind, and sense it." Her cheeks went hot. "You knew my thoughts, didn't you?"

A corner of his mouth lifted in a cocky grin in response. "I knew ye would welcome my kiss."

Cassandra pressed her lips together at the still-warm sensation tingling over her mouth.

"I know ye crave more still." His gaze rose from the ground and met hers. "How did ye make the earth sing? Is that what ye can do?"

~

FERGUS DIDN'T NEED the woman's answer spoken aloud when her thoughts registered the answer for him. They came at him in a vivid rush.

*She'd always had a connection to the earth. That, and her entire body burned with mortification that he had read her thoughts in that intimate embrace. She didn't like that she didn't know his name.*

"I'm Fergus the Undefeated," he offered. "I would offer to stymie my ability to read yer thoughts if I thought the stone was safe from ye. Cassandra." He found the name in her mind and let it grace his tongue.

The flush to her cheeks reddened further still. *He made her feel exposed.*

"Verra well," he acquiesced. "I willna search yer mind, but know I will sense any attack ye plan, aye?"

Her shoulders relaxed and a cool sense of relief washed toward him.

"I need the stone, but I do not want to fight you," she said. "You have to understand that in keeping it in your care, you will destroy Scotland."

Unease gripped Fergus. Was that why King Edgar wanted the stone? To see Scotland destroyed? But why would any king want his country left in ruin?

"I need it," Fergus said at last.

"Your need is greater than the good of Scotland?" Her brows lifted.

This lass had a feistiness to her for being such a wee bit of a thing.

"I need it to save my son," he replied earnestly.

Her brows drew together. He didn't need to read minds to know she was unsure if she ought to trust him or not. In truth, she should not. But he needed her to accompany him and would tell her anything necessary to ensure her compliance.

"He's unwell. The stone will aid him and then ye may have it when I'm done." The lie sat sourly in Fergus' mouth. He had to have her with him. Damn it, he had to have his son back.

"Why not give it to me now?" She held out her hand, as though she anticipated he might actually drop it into the softness of her slender palm.

"I know how badly ye want the stone and I canna trust that ye willna run off with it."

Her hand folded closed. "Very well, but you must allow me to travel with you."

He nodded slowly, as though he were conceding to her request. As though he didn't have to have her at his side. "Ye may travel with me. I go to Edinburgh where my son is." Guilt squeezed at him even as the darkness within him crowded at the barriers he'd erected long ago. He ought to let it in, to embrace the cold detachment it would provide. Part of him was afraid of how much it would control him, and part of him could not allow all his mother's hard work to be destroyed.

Cassandra nodded firmly, clearly assuming the matter was settled, assuming herself the victor in the discussion. Only she had no idea how terribly she had lost.

She unfurled her own bedroll across from his, on the other side of the fire. Outside the cave, lightning flickered and the roar of a fresh rainstorm sounded.

Despite their exhaustion, the night dragged on in restlessness, more in wakeful wariness than sleep, each not fully trusting the other. For his part, Fergus could rely on his heightened awareness. She would never sneak an attack upon him. However, her presence left him unnerved.

It had been years since he craved a woman at his side, over a decade. Not since Allisandre.

Mayhap it was Cassandra's incredible beauty, or the fascination of her being a Protector. Certainly it had something to do with the sweetness of her scent and how badly she made him long for her. Even as he lay opposite, his arms ached to hold her. His eyes refused to close, instead wandering repeatedly toward her smooth face, relaxed in slumber beneath the flickering light of the fire's embers.

At long last, the effects of weariness won out over his thoughts and he gave in to the quiet lull of sleep.

*They came in the night, the cowardly bastards, and pulled Allisandre from his arms. The stink of magic hung thick in the air. It clogged in his throat and rendered him frozen in place. The soldiers were quick, sent with purpose, their deeds executed with precision. They clearly had been imbued with a darkness that left their movements unnatural and sent Fergus' heart pumping like a dog on a hunt. Only when they'd jerked her from him did the magical binding break and Fergus was freed to snatch the dagger from beneath the mattress.*

*Allisandre screamed, a terrified cry that cut him to his soul. She writhed in their shadowy grips, her body swollen with Fergus' child, her bright red hair streaming about her like fire.*

*There were too many of them and Fergus' body would not obey as quickly as was necessary. It was as though he moved through a bog. Even the sharpness of his senses were dulled, save for the acute agony of loss.*

*There hadn't been a damn thing Fergus could do to protect his pregnant wife. Nay, they had dragged her from him as he watched, helplessly. He had lost everything.*

The air shifted, and the scent of magic prickled his nostrils like an impending rainstorm. The intent of movement drew his awareness with the beginnings of an attack. Fergus grasped the dagger from under his pillow and threw it with all his might at whoever planned to attack him. His actions were so fast, his target would never have been able to dodge the lethal blow.

He did not open his eyes, not wanting to see Allisandre being dragged away in the moonlight again. Then another scent appeared beneath the foulness of magic and made his eyes fly open. Apples. Sweet and fresh.

Cassandra.

He sat up, fully awake, painfully aware. Her ragged breath pulled his attention to where she sat against the rough cave wall, her eyes open wide in shock with the dagger caught between her hands.

## CHAPTER 5

Cassandra stared at the tip of the dagger, barely one inch from her face. Had she not had the skill and strength to catch it, the wicked blade would have soared straight through her head.

"Cassandra." Fergus called to her in a hoarse voice.

She ought to have been afraid. Her heart surely should race with her death defying catch and how close she was to her own mortality. Yet her hand was steady as she lowered the blade and regarded Fergus. "You threw a knife at my head."

"No' with intention."

"You have tremendous aim without intention." She rose to her feet and handed the dagger to him.

His fingers closed over the hilt and brushed her own. His thoughts poured into her.

*He was afraid. Not only of having almost killed her, for she was too important to lose, but also from the magic in the air.*

She drew in a deep inhale and recognized the prickling scent of magic from his mind. "You don't like magic. Why not?"

He grasped the hilt more firmly and snatched it out of her hands. "It's nearly dawn."

It was no answer. Frustration tightened through her shoulders. "Why do you worry at having almost killed me?" she asked. "I was under the impression we were supposed to fight one another to our dying breaths."

The lines on his brow creased with intense concentration while he pointedly ignored her. He crouched beside where he slept and rolled his bedding into a neat bundle.

"Are we supposed to fight?" she pressed.

He glared up at her. "We should go."

The magic still lingered in the air, a cool, wet scent. "Where did the magic come from?"

He shot to his feet and glowered at her. "Why do ye ask so many damn questions?"

She stood her ground. "Because you're not answering a single one."

His eyes narrowed. "I almost killed ye."

"I'm not so easily slain." She folded her arms over her chest. "Why do you hate magic?"

"Nothing good ever comes from it." He scooped a handful of water from the small bowl by the fire and splashed it over his face. It dripped from his dark beard. "Maybe ye should be asking, because I haven't an idea."

"The stone is magic," Cassandra pointed out.

He scrubbed a linen over his face. "It's different."

A gray light cast toward the back wall of the small cave, indicating the sun had begun to rise. There would be no point in attempting to go back to sleep.

"We wouldna be here if it werena for this stone." His lip lifted with disgust and his gaze wandered down to his chest where the lump of the stone lay beneath the chain mail he'd slept in.

If she'd had chain mail, she would have slept in it too. "Let me have it."

He smirked. "Is it no' enough ye draw from its power by being near?"

She tried to tamp down the swell of impatience. It would not get her the stone any faster. And he could sense every emotion threading through her.

"It is dangerous for you to keep." She spoke quietly in an attempt to leverage her patience. "You will destroy all of Scotland if it remains in your care."

His somber expression darkened. "Because magic is a terrible thing. Even earthy magic like this."

"That magic will save your son."

She thought he might not have an argument against that. But he turned his head to the side and said, "Magic stole my wife."

He hefted his packs and strode from the cave. Cassandra hurriedly assembled her own effects. A wild chill rent down her spine. She couldn't lose him. She couldn't lose the stone.

The hard packed dirt floor gave way to mud as Cassandra neared the mouth of the cave. Rain continued to pour down without respite. The horses had been tucked beneath a stone ledge that acted as a crude shelter over their heads. If nothing else, it had kept them relatively dry.

Fergus stood beside his horse, tying the packs into place behind his heavy saddle. Phillip had a similar leather seat, reinforced with a pommel to keep him locked into place despite the weight of his chain mail, and studded with metal to offer protection with the luxury befitting a knight.

The thought of her brother seemed like recalling another life, one a world away without hunger and rain, where she had a warm bed and the worst of her troubles was her family's heavy expectation. Phillip's broad smile radiated in her mind and left her heart aching for him and his constant instructions. She missed the comforts of home, but more than anything, she missed her brother.

The rain came down with such terrible might, any conversation between her and Fergus was impossible. Which was well and good, for it did not appear Fergus wished to speak. Indeed nor did she. Not when her soul was pained with the loss of everything she missed.

Together the miserable pair of them staggered through the storm, enduring the downpour as it pelted them with enough force to sting the exposed skin on their cheeks and hands. Their progress was painstakingly slow and the shoreline of the Isle of Skye took the better part of three hours to appear when it ought to have taken a third of the time.

Lightning streaked across the sky and flickered a brilliant light over them. Cassandra turned her face from the ominous sky and regarded Fergus. "We should wait for the storm to pass."

He shook his head and pushed his horse onward to the gravel shore where a lone birlinn lay on its side. The vessel was crude, fashioned from a wooden hull with oars set beneath the narrow row of seats. Fergus hopped down from his horse and approached the simple boat.

The water ahead, their necessary path for quitting the island and making their way back to land, churned and roiled with wild, erratic waves swelling from all angles without any predictable pattern. Cassandra was no sailor, but even she knew navigating such waters would be impossible. "No one will ferry us across. Not today."

"I dinna expect they will." Fergus spoke loudly to be heard over the storm. He made his way back to his horse and removed his packs.

Cassandra watched him warily. "We will not be able to take the horses." Nor did the birlinn belong to them. She could not help but assume it most likely belonged to a simple fisherman, one whose livelihood no doubt depended on the small boat.

"We'll no' be taking the horses." He motioned for her to remove her items from her horse. "They'll be payment for the birlinn."

Within minutes, he had approached a small home in the distance and negotiated possession of the vessel from an overjoyed man who gladly traded the boat for the quality horseflesh he received in return. Securing the vessel though was only the smaller part of their victory. They still had to survive the crossing.

~

THE WAVES WASHED over the sides of the simple boat and sloshed against them. Fergus and Cassandra were drenched, both from the splash of seawater and the deluge still raining down from above. Fergus rowed with all his might, but the birlinn seemed no further from the shore than it had been half an hour before.

Lightning flashed, followed by a crack of thunder so loud, it made their boat vibrate. Fergus' stomach rolled with the waves, knocking and swirling until sweat formed beneath the layers of rain and seawater.

"Let me take the oars," Cassandra shouted.

It was on the tip of Fergus' tongue to refuse to allow a lady to head the rowing. But his stomach lurched in protest of doing anything more than cradling the offending bit of his body and wishing for relief however that might come. He shoved the oars in her direction.

Their hands briefly touched and strength whispered between them. It bolstered his countenance with a reserve he would not have otherwise had. She gripped the oars and drew her body back in a hearty row. The boat bobbed over the waves and glided further from the shore. Several more rows and they were finally making headway through the terrible might of the storm.

Even still as they rowed onward, the helplessness to the violent swaying gripped Fergus once more. His entire world swayed and his body was suddenly too feeble to keep him upright. A formidable wave slammed into the boat and delivered upon them a savage knock to the right. Fergus' body lulled limp to the edge and teetered over the water for a brief moment.

A strong hand grasped his wrist and jerked him back. Again, the strength soared between them, and drove away the debilitating effects of his weakness. But he was not the only one to feel something from their connection.

Power roared through Cassandra's veins and cast a calm through her soul. The stone called to her. He could hear it over the noise of the storm, and his own illness.

*She did not know what to do with it. Frustration balled within her and rippled the calm.*

Fergus remembered that very irritation when he'd first come into his ability. Not truly understanding it, yet knowing it was there. "Close yer eyes," he ground out.

She closed her eyes, her hand still locked about his wrist. He grasped her other hand with his free one and locked their connection. Her strength hummed through his veins and the storm's roar intensified with her connection to the earth. The sea beneath them pulsed with a thundering heartbeat as though it were locked in battle, and the wind sang in his ears. How did she manage living in such chaos?

He could sense her searching the link between them, testing it, testing him. A shudder wracked through him and a wall went up in his mind to block her from his thoughts. With their shared power, he would need to always be vigilant to keep her from knowing his mind.

Instead, he sent out memories of his own experiences. The way he had learned to tame it over the years, to groom it into submission so he was no longer at its mercy.

Cassandra released one of his hands and stretched her palm out over the water. The energy between them welled and drained from him toward her. Her fingers trembled.

The waves surrounding their boat calmed to a gentle lapping at the sides of the birlinn. Everywhere else, the water roiled and churned and spit angrily at them, yet their vessel remained in place.

*Disbelief threatened to overwhelm Cassandra. This was more than she ever thought possible of herself.*

And yet she could do so, so much more. Fergus could sense it simmering under the surface of her doubt, like a pot ready to boil over. Only she would have to find it for herself. He knew as much from experience with himself.

Allisandre had known about his skills and encouraged him with them, driving him to push harder and concentrate more. Those sessions had never been helpful and had ended with Fergus exhausted and frustrated, with ripples of disappointment flowing off Allisandre.

He would not do the same now to Cassandra.

They remained stationary in the calm water. Fergus' body, however, continued to suffer the effects of the brutal waves, even though they no longer pummeled against the birlinn. His stomach clenched mercilessly and made him grateful he had not broken his fast yet that day.

*Cassandra realized his plight and could not herself row the boat while concentrating on her abilities. She needed her other hand.*

Fergus released her hand. The connection cut immediately between them and the boat pitched violently in the water, nearly tumbling them both overboard. His hands shot out and clasped her waist to steady her, to connect them once more.

Energy hummed and crackled again, flowing from the stone and through Fergus to Cassandra.

The sea settled near their vessel even as the storm raged overhead. She carefully put out her left hand on the other side of the boat and swept her fingers gracefully forward. The boat glided toward their destined shore, nudged speedily along by ripples of currents beneath the still water beneath them.

He was impressed. Thoroughly so. She had grappled her talents and put them to immediate use. The warmth of her flattered pleasure washed over him, and he knew she heard his praising thoughts.

His other thoughts, though, he continued to keep walled up. The ones of his fear for his son, the truth of his ultimate impending deception of Cassandra, and even the surge of desire gripping him as he held her narrow waist. The warmth of her skin heated his palms through her wet kirtle and her ribs flexed and swelled with each breath. She was life against his touch, slender and beautiful.

They neared the shore when the boat began to slow and began to rock hard from side to side once more. Cassandra's hands lowered slightly and her weight sagged against his hold. Her energy was faltering. But then, she was not accustomed to so fully applying her ability. She flicked her hands forward and a mighty wave crashed into the back of the birlinn. The boat slid quickly over the water and did not stop until it bounced against the rocky shore.

Despite his own weakness and the churning of his stomach, Fergus drew her in his arms along with their packs and hopped from the boat, lest they be pulled back out into the violent sea.

For surely, they might not survive a second time. He staggered to the shoreline, set Cassandra to her feet, and collapsed to his knees, heedless of the sharp stones biting through his surcoat and woolen hose and the icy water lapping over his feet.

Cassandra pulled the packs from his arms and hefted the incredible weight into her thin arms without issue despite her exhaustion.

She set them gingerly on the sandy shore and dug through her pack until she produced a twisted root. Using the edge of her blade, she scraped away the smooth brown bark and presented him with a sliver of yellow white root. "Chew on this. It will settle your stomach."

He accepted it and obediently popped it in his mouth. It was spicy and wet against his tongue and produced a sharp juice when he bit down upon it. True to her word, after several minutes, the discomfort passed and he was able to rise to his feet without the world swaying about him.

Cassandra was weak, evidenced by the waning of her arcing energy. Fergus was as well, sapped by the weakness of his body after the violent crossing. They may be on dry land and he may be standing, but they needed shelter to recover or they'd be vulnerable to any kind of attack.

Fergus set his hand to the stone at his chest. Its warmth radiated against his palm, ensuring him of its presence. He couldn't do anything to risk the loss of this stone, not when his son awaited him. There was too much to lose.

# CHAPTER 6

Shelter was a necessary need. Fortunately, there were several homes near the shore, one of which even opened their door to Fergus. The eye and nose peering with wary curiosity through a slender crack had instructed them toward an inn a furlong or so away. Indeed, they found the aged building with a slight right lean to it, and were able to secure a room until the following morning.

It had been Fergus' intent to provide an additional room for Cassandra, out of respect. However, he sensed fear spike in her at the thought of being away from him. She still did not trust him.

While he could not blame her cautious regard, he did not like it.

After getting a plate of hearty stew for Cassandra and a bit of bread and ale to further ease his own stomach, Fergus led her from the common room up the dark, narrow stairs to the row of rented rooms above. His legs were heavy as lead and his entire body seemed to sag under the burden of exhaustion. Still, he stayed near Cassandra's side should she need him for support. The feat of getting them over the water had greatly taxed her strength and the energy around her wavered like a candle near the end of its wick.

Inside their room, the innkeeper's wife was tying off a string against one side of the wall, so it draped in front of the fireplace. She tugged it with her reddened fingers and turned her cheerful face in their direction. There was a sweetness emanating from her, genuine and kind, the sort he'd only seen in his mother.

"Ach, ye ate faster than I thought ye would." The innkeeper's wife wiped her hands on the skirt of her kirtle in a manner which seemed more habit than necessity. "Ye looked as though ye might need dry things, so I brought ye some of our clothes to wear while ye set yers by the fire." She looked down at herself then to Cassandra and flushed. "I'm no' the wisp of a lass I once was, mind ye, and my husband is no' so braw as ye." Her gaze crept up to Fergus' chest and shoulders. The flush deepened and Fergus intentionally kept himself from her thoughts. "But they'll do fine." She hummed in confirmation to herself. "Aye, fine enough. If ye need anything further, dinna hesitate to give a call."

"That was kind of you, thank you." Cassandra smiled at the woman who nodded briskly, wiped her hands upon her kirtle once more, and departed the room.

On the bed lay two simple tunics, both made of rough wool, as well as two undergarments of linen. It was indeed a kindness for their hosts to bestow upon them when people of their financial standing most likely owned only a few items of clothing.

"We ought to change lest we fall ill." Cassandra set her packs down and stepped toward him. "Do you need assistance with your chain mail?"

God's teeth, did she mean to help undress him? His groin tightened at the very thought.

"I assisted my brother with his chain mail often." She put a hand to where the armor lay heavy against his shoulder. "I do not mind."

"Yer brother is a knight?" He shifted his arms upward and knelt to allow her the ability to draw the bulk of metal away.

"Aye, same as my father."

The weighty mail was lifted off and the rings clinked loudly against one another as she carefully set it aside. She was a knight's daughter. One whose brother had earned the honor as well. She was no simple peasant, though he'd known that from her noble manner of speech and the pride with which she carried herself.

She turned back toward him and scoffed. "You needn't look at me like that."

He raised his brows, pretending he could not sense her thoughts. Keeping himself from hearing her was significantly more difficult than he had anticipated. After a lifetime of being open to the emotions and thoughts of others, it was almost impossible to close it off, especially when his powers were so heightened by the grace of the stone.

*She didn't want him feeling guilty about being in this room alone with her, for having held her waist on the birlinn. For having kissed her. She had liked it far too much to regret it herself.*

"I'm the youngest daughter of three," she said. "Even if I had not been born under the burden of Protector, marriage would be difficult to obtain unless it was to a local shopkeeper."

Sensual heat radiated off her. He tried to keep his body from responding, for it was more than the energy they shared between them. There was also the simmering heat of attraction, a drawing of two bodies toward one another with the sizzling promise of consensual passion.

"I shall turn my back while ye undress," he said.

She pressed her red lips together and nodded.

*Disappointed.*

He spun away and tugged at the wet wool of his surcoat to peel it away from his linens beneath. His phallus beat with the healthy thrum of his heartbeat, wanting. He tossed the surcoat to the floor with a wet slap. A similar sound came from behind him where Cassandra undressed likewise. He imagined her, slender and milky white.

His cock hardened.

*She wanted him to come to her. There was a frustrating heat between her legs she knew he could ease. She tried to summon an image of his body without clothing but her innocent mind had no reference. She wanted to see, to know, to touch and feel.*

He clenched his hands into fists. He could take her. Right now. The temptation was great and it had been so damn long. But she was a maiden. He squeezed his fists so his closely cropped fingernails bit into his palms and reminded himself how he had failed Allisandre.

He summoned a mental wall to block her lusty thoughts and put it in front of his own to keep his thoughts from being read by her when they touched. The effort caused sweat to prickle his brow despite the wet chill settling over his skin. A worthy effort, for the sound of her thoughts went silent at long last.

"Oh." Cassandra's voice startled him from the depth of his concentration. "You are not...dressed yet...I had assumed..." Her stammered words were breathy and disjointed. Clearly she was distracted.

Fergus snatched up the linen and threw it over his head. The underclothes barely reached his knees. The tunic fell similarly short and both stretched tight over his shoulders.

He turned to Cassandra with an apology on his lips and found her slender body lost in a tent of fabric, her tunic as large as his was small. Her shapely calves were visible below the hem where her clothing fell short as his did.

Her gaze slid over him and he did not need to read her mind

to know she was seeing what lay beneath the cloth, her innocent interest lit. His body reacted with an eagerness to sate that curiosity, as well as other necessary needs they both shared.

Her hair was still wet and hung in limp curls down her shoulders, some falling down her back, the rest spilling over her chest where it parted over her breasts. The loose fabric did not offer any support to her breasts and left her pert nipples jutting from under the fabric. He wondered if her skin was still cold, if those pink buds would be cool and hard against his tongue while he heated her flesh with his mouth.

"Tell me about your wife," she said softly.

Her request jarred him from his lusty thoughts and guilt slammed hard into him. He busied himself with picking up his clothing to hang on the string set before the fire.

"I need to know," Cassandra said.

"Why?" he asked through gritted teeth. "Why must ye know?"

She lifted her wet kirtle and placed it over the hanging line by the fire. The move was nonchalant, but the gaze she slid him from the corner of her eyes was not. "I would not want to attempt to lay claim to any woman's husband."

∼

THE ADMISSION of desire ought to have embarrassed Cassandra, but it did not. Her longing was too great. Fergus put his back to her while he hung up his surcoat on the line.

She recalled all too well every inch of his naked body. His dark hair hanging down the broad expanse of his back, shadowed with muscle. The strength of his legs and his firm arse. It had made her mouth go dry to see him thus and she could not clear it from her mind. She had no wish to clear it from her mind.

He turned slowly to her. His wife was gone is what he'd said before. Did that mean she had left their home as people sometimes did? That she was dead?

Cassandra had been truthful when she'd said she didn't want to lay claim to any woman's husband. And with every molten drop of blood thundering through her veins, she wanted him.

"She's dead." He lifted his hose from the ground and draped them over the string.

Cassandra followed likewise, helping him put up his clothing beside her own kirtle. "Because of magic."

"Aye. Over ten years ago." His jaw clenched.

An ache settled in Cassandra's chest. If ten years had passed and he still mourned her, the affection between them must have been strong. "You must have loved her," she offered weakly.

Immediately she regretted having said such words. She did not want to hear of his love for his wife, no matter how foolish it made her.

His brows furrowed and the creased lines of perpetual worry there deepened. "She understood me," he answered slowly. "And I failed her."

"What did magic have to do with it?" Cassandra was pressing now, practically begging for information, and yet she could not stop herself. This girlish infatuation with the dark knight, the man tied to the same fate as she, the draw between them, was too great to ignore. It wasn't just that she wanted him. She *needed* him. The way one needed air.

He gazed down at her with his dark eyes and all the emotion roiling within. His hand lifted, palm up in silent invitation. He wanted her to touch him.

She lifted her fingers and their skin touched. Power shot through them both, firing through their veins simultaneously.

The memory swirled through her and consumed her

thoughts. *The crackle of magic, the helplessness, Allisandre's scream while she clutched her belly. The hard look of accusation as she was dragged away.* She blamed him.

Cassandra blinked and stared up into Fergus' eyes with understanding of what made him hurt.

"It wasn't your fault." She squeezed his hand. "There was nothing you could have done."

"I failed her." The force of his disappointment blazed through her. It wasn't love that cradled her to his soul, it was guilt.

His brow furrowed with pained concentration. "She's dead because of me."

"That was your son in her womb. And now he's ill."

Fergus pulled his hand from hers. "Aye." He backed away from her, as though he meant to put as much distance between himself and the conversation as possible. "She died where they held her, after having given birth to him."

"I will do anything to help you save him," Cassandra vowed. "Anything."

He looked away and she wished they were touching so she could read his thoughts. How she envied his ability.

"It isna always good to read minds," he replied. "I canna keep from doing it. They fill my thoughts even when I dinna want them to."

"Could you read my thoughts earlier?" she asked.

"Earlier," he said in a gruff tone. "In the birlinn."

"More recent than that." She let her memory glide back to the image of him naked, to the heat of her desire even as her body had been so cold while she'd dressed. How she had wanted nothing more than for him to come to her, to touch her.

Her nipples were pleasantly hard and the rasp of the rough fabric against them caused sensitive little ripples of delight. The intimate place between her legs pulsed with mind-numbing need. She wanted his mouth on hers again. She wanted to see the front of his body, to touch it, to explore what the energy they shared between them might do when they were mated together.

"I can hear yer thoughts now," he said tightly.

*Touch me. Kiss me. Satisfy this ache within me.* She called out to him with her mind. She willed him to take her and yet he did not move.

The cold shame of realization washed over her. He may not want. Her burgeoning confidence wobbled. How foolish to have not even considered—

"Ye're a maiden, Cassandra." His gaze raked over the massive dress she wore and settled on her breasts. "Ye're a knight's daughter." There was more. Something he wasn't saying.

"I have no hope for an advantageous marriage as my sisters do, nor do I desire one. This is my path. It has always been my path."

"Cassandra." Her name came out in a growl.

"The stone and us, we are tied together as one." She put her hands to his chest.

*He knew he would fail her too.*

Cassandra shook her head. "You won't fail me."

The thought disappeared and the fire of lust took its place, white hot and ravenous. His heartbeat thundered under her fingertips. She stared up in his eyes, lost in the dark depths there, drawn into his power and the force of their desire.

"If I kiss ye, I willna be able to stop." His lust was only barely restrained. She could sense the difficulty he had in maintaining himself even now, and she pried against it with her own will, her own want.

He cupped the back of her head in his large palm and tilted her face up to his. "Ye undo me, Cassandra." His mouth lowered to hers and he kissed her with all the heat of his desire.

## CHAPTER 7

Cassandra's world lit in the glow of raw energy mingling with beautiful passion. Her own yearning melded with his and roared between them. He caught her more tightly against him and slanted his mouth over hers.

His tongue swept between the seam of her lips, as it had done before, as she'd fantasized about since. She licked at his mouth, eager to match the pleasure he gave. Not only did he like it, she sensed his anticipation as tangibly as her own.

Her hands still rested against his chest, her palms humming with the strength wavering off the stone and whirling about them like brilliant starlight. His mouth ravaged hers in the most delicious of ways. His lips ground against hers, as though he wanted to consume all of her with their kiss. But she knew there was more to what they did than a kiss. She could feel it in the heaviness of her breasts, the heat pulsing between her legs, the hardness of his groin straining against her stomach.

He broke off their kiss and stared down at her with glittering black eyes. His lip curled in a lopsided smile, arrogant and so handsome it caught her breath. "Ach, aye, lass. There is much, much more."

He ran his thumb over her mouth, still tingling from their shared kisses, and ran the digit down her throat. He lowered his head and pressed his lips to her neck. The skin there was far more sensitive than she'd ever realized. Her whole body prickled to life at the simple, intimate kiss. She cradled him in her arms and curled him closer to her.

His hands skimmed down her shoulder, over her back and to the sides of her breasts. She moaned with an innate need and thrust her chest forward. He groaned and swept a finger over her nipple. Sharp pleasure shot through her and she sucked in a breath.

His beard rasped against her neck while the heat of his mouth trailed from her earlobe to the juncture between her shoulders and neck, and down to her neckline. He massaged her breasts in his palms and the blunt ends of his fingers circled the hard points of her nipples, again and again and again until she thought she might die of want.

He chuckled. "Impatient."

Cassandra closed her eyes and focused on the energy between them. She found the thread of his lust and followed its source to what he longed for. Her fingers raked down his chest past where his tight stomach flexed with each hard breath, and to the rigid staff jutting against her.

He hissed an exhale between his teeth and his hips jerked. Sexual delight sizzled through him and filtered through her by her touch. She molded her fingers around the hard bulk, measuring and teasing all at once. He thrust forward and his eyes closed in obvious enjoyment.

She nuzzled his ear, the way he'd done with her and spoke against his ear lobe so her breath whispered hot against his skin. "Who is impatient now?"

He grasped her bottom with both hands and the hem of her skirt lifted. The chilled air of the room swept over her knees.

She grasped his shoulders to keep from falling while her world spun. He settled her pelvis against his and the hard length of his maleness nudged against her center.

She gave a little cry without meaning to. A flicker of arrogant pride flitted through him and she might have cast him a teasing chastisement had he not taken that moment to rub against her intimate place once more.

The friction built a decadent heat to what was already warm and aching. She found herself arching against him in a helpless rhythm that only seemed to leave her more frustrated.

*Please.*

Though she said it only in her mind, his eyes lit with intent. He fisted the fabric at her bottom and raked his hands upward, drawing the tunic and the linen together in one fluid sweep that left her entirely nude. The sudden loss of their touch, their connection, rendered her bereft and alone.

Cassandra's body heated at the vulnerable exposure and her hands lifted to cover herself. Fergus took her hands and shook his head without ever drawing his gaze from her.

With that simple, innocent touch came a barrage of his thoughts. How perfectly lovely he found her. *A goddess.*

She flushed and had only begun to think how she longed to see him when he jerked the hem of his tunic over his head. The breath fled Cassandra's lungs and every bit of moisture fled her mouth. She shifted her legs together, discovering where the wetness in her body had gone in a pulsing madness of need.

Fergus' back had been glorious and impressive. But the front of him...

Cassandra's mouth parted in awe. The massive span of his shoulders rippled with strength that ran over his powerful chest. His stomach clenched with bands of muscles with each breath. The stone was a deep green gem which hung from a gilded chain against his chest. Her gaze lingered there briefly before curiosity drove her onward. A sprinkling of dark hair covered his torso and ran in a tantalizing line from the indent of his navel.

On his hip, the opposite one of her own, was the mark of a dagger, pointing the other direction. Her match. She gasped and met his eye. He nodded in silent agreement. "We are both bound to the stone. To each other."

She put her hand to her own hip and let her fingertip skim over the mark there. Even as she caressed it, curiosity pulled her stare lower still, down, down, down to—

She jerked her gaze away. The column of desire she'd felt beneath the tunic had seemed large, but not quite so long, nor so…alive. It ticked in time with his heartbeat, the head massively swollen as though it were to the point of bursting.

"It's a flattering assessment," he said playfully. "But I assure ye, I'll keep it from bursting until I've felt ye climax around me."

She lifted her curious stare to him once more. Up his sculpted calves, over the strength of his thighs to where the patch of dark, curling hair embraced the base of his phallus. Fear snagged at the back of her mind and warred with desire.

At least until Fergus touched his fingertips to her chin, just below her lips.

*He would be gentle. Loving. The way she deserved. He wanted to please her. With his hands. His mouth. His cock.*

She gasped softly at the vulgar word and yet her yearning intensified. He pulled her lower lip down slightly and then kissed her with reserved hunger. She didn't want this gentleness from him. She nipped at his mouth and arced her tongue against his to encourage a battle of lust.

He growled, a sound which vibrated through her and hummed at her core. The energy soared between them, bright with the promise of sated satisfaction, an end to the drive of sexual frustration. He cupped her breast and toyed with the nipple as he had before. Without warning and so quickly she did not anticipate his movement, he lowered his head over her breast and pulled one pink bud into the heat of his mouth, suckling. A needling pleasure prickled through her.

She cried out, her voice husky. He secured her to him with his arm about her lower back and walked the fingers of his free hand down from her breast, past her navel to where she burned for his touch. He licked her nipple, slowly at first with the flat of his tongue before circling it and flicking it repeatedly before finally sucking it between his lips once more.

Finally, when she was nearly mad with his caresses, he clasped her thigh and drew her leg over his hip. His skin was hot against hers, the hair of the back of his legs prickly where it brushed her calf and heel. Something blunt brushed the juncture between her legs, hard and hot.

Fergus' body tensed and she sensed the restraint in him become far more difficult to maintain. She pushed her hips forward so the edge of him pushed against her. Their marks overlapped one another, his pointing to the right, hers pointed to the left. Heat fissured between them and raced through their blood.

His arm at her back tightened. The stone pressed between them and threatened to burn Cassandra's skin where its weight bore into her. A headiness robbed her of breath, though she could not tell if it was the stone, or if it was Fergus.

"No' yet." He paused to breathe, and she knew with her heightened awareness they shared that he needed the moment to reclaim his control.

And yet so much of her wanted to shatter it.

His free hand brushed against her inner thigh, caressing while drifting higher up, closer and closer to the heat throbbing between her legs.

"Yer want is making this so damn impossible," he said in a

ragged voice. "Knowing how bad ye want me." He gritted his teeth. "How bloody bad I want ye."

His fingers skimmed between her thighs and pleasure threatened to tear her apart, the combination of hers and the power of his. He bowed his head over her and captured her mouth with his as his fingers stroked and stroked and stroked until she cried out with blind need against his lips.

When she thought she could stand the teasing no more, he swept her standing leg from her and wrapped her legs around his waist, carrying her to the bed and carefully lowering them both to the soft surface. His eyes bore down into her, lit with promise and lust and true temptation. Soon this man would lay claim to her and she to him, and their energy would be completely joined in its full magnificence.

∼

FERGUS COULD SCARCELY THINK over the mindlessness of his yearning. As if it were not already bad enough for him to control himself, the frantic, desperate thoughts of Cassandra pouring into his mind only served to weaken his wavering resolve.

He wanted to hold down her hands, trapping her willingly beneath him and drive deep and hard into her. But she was a maiden. She needed to be prepared.

Her hips arched in the natural rhythm of sex, enticing him toward her. God's bones, she would be her own undoing with such movements. Her breasts strained upward, the nipples pink and hard from his ministrations. His mouth watered to close over them again and suckle until her breathy moans filled the small room.

He shifted his hand between them once more so his fingers glided over her slick center. Her body was ready for him, eager for him.

*More. She wanted more.*

And God how he longed to give her so much more. He nudged the end of his middle finger against her entrance and carefully inserted it within her. She gave a soft exclamation of encouragement.

*More.*

Her sheath gripped him tightly. So damn tightly. Sweat warmed his brow and lower back. His cock strained ferociously between them. He moved his finger within her, gentle in his attempt to stretch her to accommodate him.

Her legs spread and greedy desperation hummed through her, a combination of her thoughts and the charge of the earth beneath them. She pushed against him.

*Please.*

He groaned his own frustration. Wanting to be inside her. Not wanting to hurt her. But God, wanting to be inside her.

In one fluid movement he did not anticipate, she grabbed his wrist, pulling him from her, and flipped him onto his back. Strength sang through his blood and he knew he could have stopped her if he wanted to. Her lips quirked up in a coquettish, confident manner.

*She was taking the control.*

Fergus lay back, pinned beneath her as she straddled his hips. His mark lay a mere inch below hers, like a shadow. He wanted them pressed together once more, pleasantly warm while their bodies ignited with shared passion. The wet heat of her entrance pressed to the underside of his shaft. He gripped the blanket in his fists to keep from lifting her up and thrusting into her. Her fingers ran over his body, lingering near the stone. He arched his hips upward, grinding their need against one another.

Her lashes fluttered and her teeth sank into her lower lip. Uncertainty wavered about her despite her show of confidence and the intent to be in charge. She was, after all, still a maiden.

He slid his hands over her thighs and held her sweet hips. "It will be easier with me above ye."

She shook her head. "Show me what to do."

He was torn at the idea of her riding him, lost somewhere between desire and fear.

"You won't hurt me," she whispered.

He hoped he did not. He focused his thoughts on showing her what to do, how to raise her hips, how to guide him in, reassuring her he would help.

She lifted her hips and curled her fingers around his shaft. His cock jerked in anticipation and his ballocks drew tight. She angled him upward so he pointed directly where he had been so hungry to enter. Then, ever so carefully, she lowered onto him.

The heat of her enveloped the sensitive head of his cock. He gave a low grunt and forced himself to lie patient and still. Cassandra sank deeper, taking in the top part of his shaft as well. She gave a sigh and he could sense her body tingle with enjoyment.

She nudged her hips up and then slowly returned to the same place. A tight groan slipped from Fergus' throat. It was all he could do to lay in place and allow her to control the pace, the depth. She continued to rock over him, each time she lowered further, and took him in deeper and deeper. Finally, she slid completely down him and the base of his phallus met the apex of her thighs.

She gripped him tightly in her sheath, almost too tightly. But it was more than his own sensations, he could feel hers as well, the way his cock stretched and filled her, the burning insistence of her body to move.

He let her rock on her own several times, her attempts clumsy with untried experience. There had been little pain for her and the delicate thrusts were becoming more desperate. Indeed, his own desires were screaming in his mind, driving him to plunge into her.

"Yes. Please." Cassandra rubbed herself with frustration over him. "Do it. The way you want. The way we both want."

He released one hand from her hips and settled his thumb against the swollen nub at the top of her sex. She drew a sharp breath. He rolled it in time with her movements, speeding when she sped. The waves of her pleasure were overwhelming, hot and delicious, especially when paired with his own experience of her gripping and gliding over his cock. Sweat beaded on his brow.

She was close. So damn close. He quickened his pace on the little bud and her panting came harder. He released her, grabbed her hips and thrust hard into her, plunging in and out. She cried out and arched her back, her small breasts bouncing each time their hips met.

Their bodies were on fire, alight with incredible passion, joined with sensations of both their experiences - gliding and slick, thick and hard, filling and stretching, squeezing, squeezing, squeezing. Her nails dug into his chest and pleasure exploded from him the same time her grip on him spasmed in her crises.

Euphoria took them to another place where they were not bound to the earth, where every nerve of their bodies flared with a bliss neither had ever known. They were joined, they were perfect. They were power. They were undefeatable.

The intensity of it was so great, it wiped clear Fergus' mind for a brief moment and dragged down the wall he had so carefully erected and maintained. Cassandra jerked to stillness atop him. He opened his eyes, still panting with the effects of their unnatural coupling.

Cassandra stared down at him with hard confusion.

He drew up the wall once more, but his correction had come too late. She had already seen into his mind. He tried to push against her thoughts, to scrape away what she knew. He searched, desperate, and discovered nothing there. Nothing but a formidable wall.

# CHAPTER 8

Cassandra knew everything, including the icy fear prickling through Fergus' veins. Being in such close proximity to him gave her the strength, the knowledge, to close the curtain of her mind and keep him from seeing her thoughts. She only hoped she possessed the strength once they were not touching, when her mind was weakened without the stone.

The coital bliss between them cooled and she climbed from his body. She left her hand resting on his chest, hesitant to remove it and lose the surge in her power. He watched her intently, his brow furrowed in hard concentration.

He wondered what she had seen in his mind, and longed to extract the knowledge from her mind. His racing heartbeat under her palm calmed to a steady thud and still she did not pull away her hand. She knew everything.

He had never seen his son, he didn't even know his name, yet still his love for the child was fierce. The king was using the boy to encourage Fergus to do his bidding. And Cassandra was part of that bidding. The king needed not only the stone, but also her.

Yet there was more, a part of Fergus going deeper than he

even realized. There was good in him. A beautiful beacon of goodness shining in the inky darkness within. He had hope - for a family, for love. And she had become part of that hope, even as he knew he would have to turn her over to the king's care. Even as he knew it would most likely end in her death.

The earth's presence crackled around Cassandra. A reminder of the strength she stood upon every day, the strength she had only just learned to draw from. She closed her eyes and pulled the buzz of energy toward her. It hummed through her veins and lit her body and mind with exactly what she needed.

She opened her eyes and removed her hand from Fergus' chest. His mind tapped against hers, and yet she maintained the control to keep him at bay.

"How do ye know how to do that?" he asked.

"A Protector's secret." She glanced over her shoulder at him. While she no longer had his ability to sense emotions wavering off anyone or read their thoughts, she could see the frustration carved on his face.

He rose from the bed, naked and obviously unashamed of his fully nude state. She was not so blissfully uncaring. Her face burned with heat. She had wanted him with a force wild enough to threaten to rip her apart, and what they had shared had been incredible.

All this time, he meant to betray her. And yet since the moment he met her, he did not want to. Every decision was for his son. Could she fault such a noble cause?

"Cassandra." He reached out to her.

She looked at his hand stretching toward her. "If you mean to read my thoughts by touching me, you will only find I have more strength."

"What did ye see?" he asked.

"Enough." She drew the clothing they'd discarded from the

ground, grabbing first Fergus' garments in error. "This is yours." She handed it to him.

He accepted the bundle and clutched it to his chest. Cassandra did not hesitate with her own clothing. She pulled the linen and wool tunic on together, the two garments still connected from where Fergus had pulled them from her body.

"I dinna want it to end like this." He took her hand in his.

"As I stated previously, you cannot read my—"

"I dinna want to read yer thoughts." He shook his head. "I mean, aye, I do, but I wanted...I wanted to touch ye. After what we experienced together."

She relented and his strong hand curled against her own.

"I want ye to stay with me," he said. "I want ye to come with me to Edinburgh."

*Truth.*

She knew his words to be true. She could sense the honesty in him through the touch of their fingers threaded together.

"To heal your son," she said.

*Guilt.*

It scored into him, white hot and ugly before he could cover it. "Aye," he answered slowly, as if he suspected she did not believe him. "To heal my son."

"What do you think I know, Fergus?" She met his gaze and he shook his head.

"I dinna know, but I dinna want ye to leave me."

*Fear.*

*Solitude.*

*So vastly empty and alone.*

She recalled the glow of hope within him, dimly lit and tucked in a corner shrouded by helplessness. He was not all darkness within. She swallowed.

But what of her path? Was she supposed to aid him? Was she supposed to fight him and take the stone? She wished her eldmother were still alive and could read her future - beyond the fate of Cassandra being a Protector and to where she was now.

If she failed in the task to obtain the stone, it was more than she who would suffer. It was all of Scotland.

"Stay with me," Fergus said gently. He lifted his free hand to her face and ran his thumb down her cheek to her chin, just below her bottom lip.

Her pulse fluttered and despite the uncertainty in her future and the understanding she had to be wary of trusting him, her body warmed with lust. Outside the rain raged against the shutters and thunder grumbled in the distance.

Even if she were to leave now, in wet clothing and amid the mighty storm, she would not have the stone. She needed a plan.

Fergus brought his face closer to hers. His mouth a breath from hers. She found herself tipping her face toward him.

He slid one large hand up the back of her neck to cradle the back of her head. "Will ye come with me?"

Cassandra stared deep into his eyes, cherishing those heady moments before their lips met "Aye."

And even as they kissed and passion ignited their veins once more, she found herself wondering if it would be she who would betray him, or he who betrayed her.

~

Several days on the road together had not provided Fergus the opportunity to fully understand what Cassandra knew. There had been a shift in her, a wariness, and yet she had so successfully erected a wall to prevent him from her thoughts, it was impenetrable. And damn impressive.

It had taken him months to learn how to properly block his mind, a skill he hadn't realized he needed to develop until his meetings with the king. Somehow the bastard always seemed to know what Fergus had been thinking in their prior meeting.

Snow dusted the ground like baker's flour, leaving dots of white mingled with the bits of wilting grass and dry heather. The air held a wet cold to it that pierced one's bones and made Fergus wish they had shared a horse rather than having their own. Though with the terrain being rough through Inverness and the ground slick in places, the animals needed to be spared. Especially when the beasts were as shoddy as they were, having been procured from a neglected stable near their inn.

Had Fergus not known the land so well from his youth, it might have been impossible to navigate.

He slid a glance to Cassandra and found her watching him, as she often did, her expression ponderous beneath the cloak wrapped about her. She was little more than a face from beneath furred hood, emitting occasional puffs of frozen air from her lips. The weather had been uncommonly cold for mid-November.

He could not read her thoughts, but he knew her emotions to be warring. They blurred about her in a confused mass, indecipherable.

There was lust, he knew. Aye, he knew that very, very well. It was a flame they handled often despite the awareness that one of them might end up burned. For there was a distinct lack of trust within her, that he knew with certainty.

They made their way down the steep side of a hill, their progress slow with the mud-thickened earth. Wind howled at them and nipped at their exposed faces.

"Do you find this weather strange?" she asked. "It has never been so cold this early before."

"You are used to being farther south." Fergus guided his horse away from a puddle, unsure how deep it might be.

"I've heard people in the villages discussing it. They have

never seen weather such as this in November either." She glanced in his direction, her stare pointed.

He knew where she was taking this conversation, where she had taken it before. The need for her to possess the stone. Yet he knew if she had it, she would leave - to ensure he never had possession of it again. Sacrificing everything for the safety of Scotland - him, what they had, and even his son.

The sacrifice of few for the survival of many.

"I canna give ye the stone," he said resolutely.

"But you must see—" The ground beneath Cassandra's horse slid away, like its skin pulled free from the slippery mud beneath. Her horse's hooves scrabbled for purchase, its mighty hindquarters thrusting against the moving earth threatening to pull it down.

Fergus nudged his horse forward in an attempt to help, but his steed lurched backward to safer ground, its baser instincts falling to preservation.

Cassandra released the reins with one hand and the force of her power swelled thick in the cold air. But without touching Fergus and pulling from the force of the stone, her strength was not enough.

She needed him. He leapt from the saddle. His feet splashed on the sodden ground and threatened to slide out from beneath him as well. Cassandra wobbled on her horse while the poor beast continued to struggle, legs racing against the earth falling away beneath them both.

"Nay, hold the reins," Fergus bellowed.

Cassandra's hand shook with the force of her concentration. Her horse lurched to the right as the ground washed away. It leapt into the air and sent Cassandra flying from its back while its hooves finally found solid ground.

She gave a brief shriek midair and somehow managed to land on her feet, which promptly gave way beneath her.

"Nay," Fergus cried. He lunged for her and caught the front of her cloak as the river of mud dragged her downward. It sucked at her with such strength, it almost drew them both to their demise. But Fergus had the stone, and he called on every last fissure of energy within it to save Cassandra.

He clutched her to his chest, unwilling to let her go when he had come so close to almost losing her.

"I am not so easily lost," Cassandra said.

He looked down and found her gazing up at him. Mud had spattered against her cheeks and her hood had fallen away, leaving her dark curls in a wild disarray. Yet never had she looked more beautiful. More his.

"And I thank God for it." He pressed a kiss to her warm, soft lips, not caring if he got mud on his own face.

Pain radiated from her and he pulled back. "Ye're hurt." He scanned over her, though it was impossible to see anything beneath the heavily furred cloak she wore.

She twisted her lips with frustration. "My ankle."

He had to see the limb, but not here where the ground might once more slide away. A desperate survey of their surroundings revealed the rounded stone entrance of what might be a cave. He lifted her into his arms and carried her to it. The horses had both given to grazing once the excitement of their near death had passed, and so he left them thus.

"It is not so bad," Cassandra said.

Rather than answer, Fergus extended his awareness into the cave in an effort to identify any creatures within. Finding none, he ducked into the low ceiling and carried her to the edge, where he could still see well enough, and set her to the dry dirt floor. Her right foot settled on the ground and she gave a hiss of pain despite her protests of being fine.

He pulled off her shoe and rolled down her thick woolen stockings to reveal her slender calf and a misshapen ankle already beginning to bloom with shapeless blotches of purple and red. Definitely not a good sign.

Cassandra lifted and lowered her foot then turned it side to side. "It hurts, but I can move it. It's not broken."

"Nay, but it still needs care. Ye need rest. And a healer." He, of course, knew the best healer in all of Scotland, though he'd been hesitant to go and see her after all these years. She hadn't liked Allisandre, yet she'd still traveled for miles to come and see him after his wife's death. He should have visited sooner, he knew, but excuses piled upon one another until he had been gone too long and remorse had prevented him from facing his wrong. Guilt had a way of settling in the soul like a stain and keeping one from doing what was right.

It would appear Cassandra's injury would finally make right that wrong from so long ago.

Fergus would finally go to see his mother.

# CHAPTER 9

It had been over a decade, yet even through the whirling snow and mounds of slushing mud, Fergus was able to find his way home. The manor sat on the outskirts of a small village, away from the bustle and noise. Exactly as his mother preferred.

A simple thatch roof cottage had once sat in its place. When Fergus was first approached by the king for help, it was within Fergus' grasp to barter for a better life. Fergus had been given wealth and had insisted his mother have a comfortable home with worthy staff. Despite everything Fergus' sacrifice afforded them, he knew his mother wished for life as it was before his mark had appeared.

He hopped down from his horse and aided Cassandra from hers. He helped her limp to the door and rapped upon it. Footsteps immediately sounded on the threshold and the door swung open, bringing with it the familiar scent of his childhood - warm baking bread and drying herbs.

The maid stared down her hawkish nose at him and gave a cold smile which only served to thin her narrow lips. Helga lifted a brow and he could read her disapproval as readily as if she'd spoken it aloud.

*Too long gone with too little care for his mother. A pity when she loved her boy so completely.*

The thought cut into his heart.

Helga's gaze shifted to where Cassandra leaned against him.

"Helga, get Mother." Fergus spoke briskly. Before the bitter woman could think something awful about Cassandra.

"She's in the kitchen," Helga replied dryly. "Of course." She widened the door to allow them to enter. He strode past her with Cassandra clutching his side for support. He'd wanted to carry her, of course, but she'd insisted on walking herself rather than being carried like an invalid.

A sense of appreciation washed from behind Fergus as Helga's gaze burned over him followed by thoughts he never wanted to hear from the old maid.

Cassandra choked on a cough and he knew she'd heard as well. Damn her. He slid her a dark gaze, but her mirthful grin didn't dissipate.

"She'll no' believe ye're hurt with the way ye're smiling," he scoffed.

"I canna imagine a lass who wouldna smile in the presence of my son." The soft voice was exactly as he remembered, kind and gentle and loving.

His heart warmed immediately, and he looked to the doorway where the voice had come from. His mother stood at the center with a wide smile on her face, her eyes crinkled with her joy.

"Ma." His heart caught.

She looked older, significantly so. Her rich golden hair had gone almost completely white with a thin, cotton-like consistency that threatened to fly free of her bun. She opened her arms and came to him, intent on the hugs she insisted she give and he insisted he was too old for.

Still supporting Cassandra on his left arm, he hugged his

mother tight to him. Her head barely came up to his ribs, at least that was the same. Her embrace was tight and full of enough love to light up the whole of Scotland. Indeed, it made his heart glow.

She held no anger at his delay in coming to see her, no sorrow at his absence, nor even frustration that he'd brought someone with him. Not his mother. She was simply glad to have her son home, because with him there, her heart was truly complete.

The idea left a knot in his throat. He had never been able to fully read his mother's thoughts, not like now with the benefit of the stone. He knew she loved him, but never had he truly understood exactly how central to her world he was.

"Are ye going to introduce me?" She glanced to Cassandra. "Surely yer mother raised ye better than that."

"This is Lady Cassandra. She is traveling with me to Edinburgh and has injured her ankle." He turned to Cassandra. "This is my mother who will provide ye with the best care of any healer or physician in all of Scotland."

"Ach, listen to him." His mother chuckled. "Ye'd think I'm a healer myself with all his praise. I'm merely a mother who sought the best care for my son when he was ill as a lad."

Despite her humble words, he could sense how his praise made her swell with pride.

She waved him toward her and turned to the kitchen. "Get her to the chair by the fire. It's warmer back here than in the drafty great hall."

Fergus followed his mother to the back of the manor where the massive kitchen was located. As they walked, he took advantage of Cassandra's slow pace to examine the state of the manor. Lucky for Helga, he found it all in good repair, polished and dusted without a cobweb to be seen.

Though he wondered how much his mother allowed Helga

to do, though, if anything at all. She had never had much use for the servants and Fergus knew she kept them more to appease him than for her own desire.

A pleasant heat filled the kitchen, even in the frigid temperatures. The entire manor belonged to his mother, yet he knew this room was the only one which seemed to truly belong to her. Herbs swayed from the rafters above, their leaves in various stages of drying, just like when they'd had a small cottage. Several jars of butters and oils were neatly lined on one side of the wall, and his father's necklace - an iron cross from when he'd traveled with the Knights Templar - hung near the shutters, just like when they'd had a small cottage. A sense of peace washed over his mother when she entered the kitchen.

Fergus set Cassandra in the wooden seat before the fire and his mother came forward to sit on a nearby stool. If anyone would make Cassandra's foot right again, it would be his mother.

"Lady Cassandra, may I remove yer shoe?" His mother regarded Cassandra with an imploring look.

Cassandra flushed. "Aye, of course, but please call me Cassandra."

His mother smiled and gently removed the shoe. Cassandra's foot had swollen even larger with a deep purple band at the base of her foot. Fergus' mother carefully examined it, her fingers gingerly moving over the swollen skin. The lines around his mother's eyes remained creased though she was no longer smiling.

Again, he was struck by how much she'd aged in ten years. He had been gone too long. She had done everything for him in his life, and he had remained gone.

He knew she would not judge him, and yet he could not bring himself to tell her about his son. And how badly he had failed.

"It's no' broken, merely a sprain," his mother offered in her assessment of Cassandra's ankle, ignorant to the waves of guilt washing over him. "But ye'll no' be moving on it for a while. I have some poultices and balms I can use to take down the engorgement and to ease yer pain a wee bit." She stood and settled a hand on his forearm where it was crossed over his chest. "Ye're of course welcome to stay here."

Her hope flared so bright, it was practically blinding. And even beneath it all, she only wanted it if Fergus could spare the time.

In truth, he could not, but Cassandra would travel more quickly when healed than she could injured. And further damage to her ankle, which was likely if they continued to press on, would only slow them even more.

They had no choice but to stay. He found himself torn between frustration at the lost time when they were already behind, and gratitude for the opportunity to spend the time with his mother. Once his son was recovered, he would ensure they moved back to Inverness along with Cassandra, near his mother's manor.

He stilled. It was the first time he had considered his future with Cassandra. The image had come so readily, with such assuredness, it was as though there were no doubt in his mind it would be.

A cold shudder rent through his heart. And yet it could not be. For he was almost certain when he delivered Cassandra to the king, she would die.

~

THE FOLLOWING week flew by quickly for Cassandra in the comfortable manor with Fergus' mother, whom she'd been instructed to refer to as Blair. Cassandra had been treated well, with all the love from Blair she had never received from her own mother, and it filled a void in her heart she hadn't known she possessed.

Blair settled comfortably on a stool with a tray at her side filled with various pots and herbs and poultices for healing. She unwrapped the linen from Cassandra's ankle and craned her neck over the injured appendage in careful assessment.

"It's almost completely healed." Blair put a hand to her chest. "I've no' ever seen a sprain as bad as yers mend with such haste."

Cassandra peered at her ankle. It was indeed as it had been before the injury, with no swelling or discoloration remaining. Fergus had constantly hovered near her in the past several days, touching his hand to hers when no one was near in the hopes the energy of the stone would encourage her body to repair itself. It was the only time he would touch her.

Even without the stone, Cassandra would no doubt have still healed well for Blair had provided constant care.

"Your diligence to my health has contributed greatly to the success, I am sure," Cassandra said.

As she always did, Blair waved a dismissive hand in the air as if to clear away the compliment. "Ye've been a fine patient to care for. Ye're a verra kind lass." Blair lifted a sly gaze to Cassandra. "And I canna say I havena noticed how my son interacts with ye."

Cassandra's face grew warm. "Whatever do you mean?"

Blair grinned and her eyes squinted at the corner where a lifetime of smiling had left the skin creased. "I see the gentle touches between ye and my son, the way his gaze seems to fix on ye when ye're near. I've no' ever seen him like this with a lass."

The warmth went hotter still. Lately it had seemed he wanted little to do with Cassandra, aside from her being ready as quickly as possible to travel. She'd tried to read his hesitation toward her but could not. At first she had assumed it had to do with his mother, and the fear she would know he had taken Cassandra's maidenhead. But several times of being alone together had cured such thoughts. Even with no one nearby, Fergus was distant. As though he had wanted to stay far from her.

"What of his wife?" Cassandra asked. Her stomach twisted at the very thought. Allisandre had possessed a part of Fergus Cassandra envied, a part of him she would never have.

Blair pursed her mouth. She lifted the lid from a small clay pot and swept her fingers through the yellow salve within. "He fancied her," she said slowly. "But there was something about her I dinna trust."

Her greased fingers moved over Cassandra's ankle, her touch tender as she massaged the salve over the remnants of the injury.

"Was his wife unkind?" Cassandra had seen, unwillingly, some of the memories in Fergus' head when they touched. While beautiful, Allisandre had seemed short of patience and possessed a cool air about her.

"She came about in Fergus' life after the king bestowed a goodly amount of wealth upon him, and was always after him to get knighted." Blair wiped the remaining balm from her fingertips. "I got the impression she liked Fergus no' for who he was, but for what he might provide her with and who he might become."

Cassandra nodded in understanding.

"Fergus needs good in his life." Blair pushed the wrapped poultice of herbs into a small bowl of water. Threads of yellow green seeped from the linen, coloring the water and filling the air with the sweet spice of herbs. "Like ye."

"Me?"

"There is a darkness in my boy." A somber note dulled the light in her eyes. "I thought it gone from him for good, but I see it now has returned. He had the very devil in him as a lad."

Fergus entered the room and both Cassandra and Blair immediately quieted. He looked between the two ladies. "Ye dinna need to stop speaking on my behalf."

"Your mother was telling me what a difficult child you were as a boy," Cassandra teased.

Fergus smirked.

"Did you have to beat it out of him?" she inquired playfully.

"Ach no." Blair rose from her seat on the low stool, moving with a fair amount of ease for one of her age. "I loved it out of him." She approached her son and drew him into a solid embrace that left his arms trapped against his body. "I cradled him in my arms and I sang him songs from my heart. I kissed away his screams and together we baked away his tantrums. He makes a fine bannock if he's ever inclined to do so for ye."

"Ma." His tone possessed a warning note the sparkle in his eye did not reflect. He liberated one of his arms only to drape it over his mother's shoulders and return the hug. An affectionate smile touched his lips, the same one he wore every time he regarded his mother.

Despite what Blair had said about Fergus having his darkness returned, Cassandra had seen a light reflecting from him when they touched. A light not present before their arrival to the manor. It was a direct mirror of the brilliance surrounding Blair, pure and beautiful. As though being in his mother's presence eased some of what weighed heavily upon him. As though her love were enough to battle every shadow of darkness away.

He gazed down at Cassandra's foot. "Ye look to be completely healed."

"Verra nearly." Blair squeezed him hard once more before releasing him. "She's mended so well." She made her way to the stool once more and pulled the poultice from where it had been steeping in the water. Pale green water dribbled from the herb-filled linen. "She'll be well enough to travel in several more days."

"Tomorrow," he said sternly.

Cassandra snapped her attention to him. "So soon?"

"We've spent too much time here." He regarded Blair and his tone softened. "Forgive me. I will return once I've gone to Edinburgh. There is something verra important I must attend to."

Blair smiled up at her son. "Of course, my son."

Without another word, Fergus quit the room, leaving a stark silence in his wake.

"I apologize for our abrupt departure," Cassandra offered meekly.

"He doesna like to leave me." Blair gazed thoughtfully to the doorway her son had strode through. "He doesna deal well with unpleasantries like farewells. But I know in my heart he loves me, and I know he will be back again someday." She set the poultice against Cassandra's ankle.

The wet heat of the herbs settled against her skin and sank deep to the injury below with a soothing heat. Blair patiently bound a linen around the ankle. "I'll include several of these poultices for ye to bring with ye as well as a pot of the ointment I've been using."

"How did you get so good at healing?" Cassandra asked.

Blair was quiet so long, Cassandra feared she had asked a question she ought not to have.

"I had a daughter once," Blair said softly. "A wee lass with blonde curls like her da and his large dark eyes. She was born a year before Fergus, but she was a sickly wee thing. She struggled for breath often and raged with fever more times than not. I'd never known much about herbs or healing. Indeed, I could scarce grow a weed." She chuckled softly at her own folly. "But I taught myself to ensure she had the best care I could provide. I learned much over the years from tending to her." Blair lifted the tray and got to her feet. "I suppose a parent will do anything for their child."

Outside a fresh storm howled and rattled at the shutters. "Ye'll need to travel with care," Blair said. "There's been a wild snowstorm raging for the better part of the week. The ground is frozen solid as a stone."

Cassandra nodded. "Thank you for everything, Blair. You've been most gracious and hospitable."

"It's been my pleasure." With that, Blair left the room with her tray of healing tools.

Cassandra stared at the flames dancing within the large hearth before her, savoring the warmth while she still had it. Tomorrow would bring the soul chilling cold once more and the journey that would end in ultimate betrayal.

Only now she had a plan. And it all started with being honest with Fergus about what she knew.

A parent might do anything to save their child, aye, but what might they be able to do with the help of another?

## CHAPTER 10

There was a dulling of the light surrounding Fergus' mother the morning of their departure. He tried to harden his heart against it, but found the task entirely impossible. Never once did she blame him for leaving, nor did she begrudge the shortness of his stay. Worse still, he sensed a fear in her that it might be the last time she would see him. It was that final thought which caused her brilliance to wane.

He pulled her into his arms and willed the understanding of all the love in his heart for her to melt into her awareness the way hers had to him. However, he was only able to receive emotion and thoughts, not send them. When he finally released her, the glow about her had not renewed any of its vigor.

"Thank you for bringing Cassandra with ye," his mother said. "I enjoyed her company greatly. I see her as being verra good for ye."

He groaned slightly and cast a glance to where Cassandra knelt near a barn cat, stroking its smooth black and orange fur.

"It's been a decade since Allisandre," his mother said gently. "I think this lass is the one to balm the soul, my son. She's a good woman."

Guilt sliced white hot through him. He hated leaving his mother, and how much it pained her for him to do so. He hated that Cassandra was exactly as his mother had said - a good woman, and he hated even more that he would betray her.

He simply nodded. "I shall take yer advice under consideration."

"Ach, consideration. Ye always were a stubborn lad," she said affectionately. "I'll miss ye."

He pulled his mother in for a final embrace and helped Cassandra to her horse after she'd said her goodbyes. His mother had insisted he take her finer horses and leave the nags behind, as she claimed she had little use for good steeds.

Wind and ice pelted at them, making any attempt at conversation arduous. He was grateful for the opportunity to remain silent. The last week had been difficult with her. He had tried to put some distance between them, a necessary amount of space for what he would have to do. He'd touched her only to help her heal and had felt her pain at his detachment.

His gaze wandered to her, simply a face inside a thick band of fur from her cloak. A beautiful face with red lips and cheeks and the tip of her nose he wanted to kiss. Damn it, he wanted to kiss all of her, to pull her into his arms.

And he would betray her. Sacrifice her.

A knot formed in his throat, a stubborn obstruction he'd found recurring in the last week. He knew the king well enough to know his intentions for Cassandra were not ones of hospitality. No doubt he would kill her.

An icy gust shoved at him and left his eyes watering with the cold. The weather was as miserable as it'd been when they started.

Fergus would do anything to protect Cassandra, sacrifice almost anything to keep her safe – except his son. He had to keep his son forefront in his mind. The lad he'd never met, the one who had waited on him all this time.

Together, he and Cassandra trudged on, their pace slowed over the frozen terrain and mounds of snow, until the sky began to darken. They stopped at a small inn within a village they were lucky enough to stumble upon. Indeed, a frozen night such as this would have been miserable in a cave. Fergus' stomach twisted at the idea of spending the night together in the same room, at the opportunity of being close without the excuse of his mother nearby and Cassandra's reputation to offer distance.

But when the innkeeper led them to their small single room with a warming fire lit in the hearth, and the sweet apple scent of her filled the room, a hunger consumed him. Unfair and insistent. It made him want to draw her slender body against him, both in lust and protection.

For there had to be something he could do. He could not give up so easily on Cassandra. Mayhap once he had his son, he could go back…

"You look so serious as you stare at me," Cassandra said.

Indeed, she looked serious too. The light was gone from her clear blue eyes. The energy arcing from her body was cast in a strange flickering, suggesting she was nervous. He made her nervous.

"Ye needn't be nervous with me," he said. "I'll no' hurt ye."

He regretted the words as soon as they fled his lips. For he would hurt her. He would betray her, perhaps too late to stop her from being killed.

His hands balled into fists. Nay, he would not let that happen.

The nervousness about her shone with more intensity.

"Then you already know," she said softly and looked away. "I thought I'd been so good at hiding it."

He frowned. "I already know what?"

"That I know."

His heartbeat faltered in his chest for a quick second before scrambling to catch the missed beat. "That ye know what?" he asked slowly.

"I know about why you need the stone and I know about your son." Her eyes were large and sad with a heavy, empathetic sorrow. "You've never met him and worry he doesn't even know you exist. You've tried to find him, but to no avail. The only way to reclaim him from where he is being held captive is to give King Edgar the stone. It's why you will not let me have it, even as the world is falling into chaos."

Fergus tried to swallow the sour bile rising in his throat. To hear all his deceit laid bare in such a manner left him feeling vulnerable in a way he never had before, completely exposed. And yet, what she had said was not the whole of it.

He should tell her the rest, to be honest. However, doing so might cause her to leave, and if she left, he would lose his son forever.

"And you have not told your mother," she continued. "About your son."

His cheeks burned with shame. "I couldna bring myself to tell her, for fear it might break her heart."

"And yours," Cassandra said softly. "To say it aloud."

Fergus gritted his teeth against the pain welling in his chest and nodded.

"Please," Cassandra implored. "Let me help you."

There was such earnestness in her gaze, such beautiful hope emanating from her, that he could not bring himself to lie to her. Not again. Not anymore.

She had to know the truth.

Cassandra's soul felt lighter for having confessed her knowledge of Fergus' son to him. However, the gray pallor to his face at her admission made her grateful she had not mentioned she knew of the betrayal.

"Ye're right," he said gravely. "But that is no' the worst of it."

She stood several feet away from him, her arms crossed over her chest to keep from reaching out to him. It was not where she wanted to be. Nay - she wanted to be in his arms, kissing him, letting him strip off her layers of clothing to press the heat of his naked body against hers. But the distance was where she needed to be.

"I know," Cassandra said through the ache in her heart.

He turned away, as though he needed the separation too. As though he could not stand to look at her, and when he spoke, she understood why. "The king doesna want only the stone. He wants ye too."

Cassandra winced at the pain in his words. "I know," she said again.

He turned to her, his brows furrowed low over his eyes as though he were in agony. "Ye knew? Ye knew and ye still traveled by my side the following day? Ye came to my mother's home and ye stayed there, ye ventured on this new part of the journey with me and are sharing a room with me, and ye knew?"

She nodded.

He gave a hoarse cry and ran his hands partway through his hair before stopping and cradling his head in his palms. "Why?" he asked in a rasping voice. "Why would ye do that?" He slid his fingers from his hair and stared desperately at her. "Why would ye stay when ye knew I most likely lead ye to yer death?"

Cassandra blinked back unexpected tears. "I...I need the stone." It was a flimsy excuse and he saw directly through it.

He shook his head.

"I couldn't leave you without your son." Cassandra looked

down at the floor, unable to meet the intensity of his bright gaze. "I intended to try to find a way to get the stone back from you while still aiding you in getting your son returned."

"And if ye failed in getting the stone?" he asked.

She lifted her head. "I won't." And it was true, she had it worked out perfectly to ensure if nothing else, the stone would remain hers.

He shook his head, as though none of it made sense to him.

But she knew exactly why she'd done it. She strode forward, reached up and cupped her hands to his face. The growth of whiskers on his jaw rasped against her palms, pleasant and intimate. The connection between them was immediate as always.

Cassandra let her wall crumple and allowed the exposure of her heart to him. She showed him what she'd learned from him, the shock of it all. She allowed him to see her desire to help him recover his son.

But there was more, so much more that she was too afraid to say. She was a coward to do it this way and yet she could not bring herself to speak such words aloud. She showed him her family and how difficult life had been growing up, and how he had made her feel accepted and cherished in a world where she was simply a pawn in the path to greatness. He celebrated her successes while others had constantly complained of her failures.

But most importantly, most pathetically, she let him understand the depth of her feelings for him. This man, who had shown her a world she had always wanted and never thought to possess, she would die for in the pursuit of getting him everything he was missing in life. Because she loved him.

Wholly, completely and most likely, foolishly.

There was only one thing she kept guarded, one small bit she couldn't share.

"Cassandra." He drew in a harsh breath. "Do not love me."

"I cannot make myself stop. Even as I knew you would betray me, I understood your cause and I love you." Saying the words aloud loosened the tight hold fear had on her. It was like throwing wide one's hands in the air and flying free. "I love you, Fergus."

"Dinna say it." He pulled his hands away, but not fast enough, not before she sensed what charged through him. Doubt. Not in her, but in himself.

He would have to believe in his worth before he accepted her love, and before he could allow himself to feel the same way.

"Let me help you," she insisted. "We can work together to save your son."

He strode to the shuttered windows and braced his hands on either side of the frame. His head hung in defeat between his shoulders. "I dinna like this."

She approached him and reached out, hungry to know what it was he thought when he was so guarded with his mind.

"I have to choose between ye or my son."

"I am not making you choose." Her arms longed to hold him. Not only for his thoughts, but for the comfort of his warmth and strength.

"Do ye no' see how much worse it is?" He straightened. "Ye are willingly walking into a trap, mayhap sacrificing yourself, for my happiness."

"You would do the same for me," she said.

He opened his arms and she stepped into his embrace. His arms were warm and strong, the embrace so comforting and rife with power, she melted against him. He nuzzled her, his lips brushing her ear.

Her body immediately lit with desire, raw and desperate. In the previous week they had touched so little, and had no time alone; she needed him like she needed air. His mouth slanted over hers and seared her with the force of his own lust.

She sensed the emotions warring within him, the worthlessness overwhelmed by want. It would all work out. She conveyed the thought to him in her mind in an attempt to share her confidence before giving herself completely to the heat of his touch and the delicious fire it ignited within her.

*I have a plan.*

# CHAPTER 11

Cassandra's plan required a week long delay in Stirling upon their arrival. After having taken almost a month to get there, the wait was a generous sacrifice. One they were not pleased with having to make. The length of time for their travel had been unheard of, even in winter as they now were.

The winds blew without cessation and the constant blend of rain and snow left all of Scotland frozen over. It was nearly two moons since Fergus had put the stone around his neck. The earth's pulse was beginning to grow weak beneath Cassandra's feet, pressing her own purpose despite her knowledge of how important Fergus' son truly was.

She hadn't realized how painful it would be to be near the stone, to tangibly understand the debilitating effects on the earth, and do nothing. There was a maternal ache in her chest, and her charge was dying. Scotland needed her.

The understanding tore into her heart and ravaged her conscience. There were times she wished she had not seen Fergus' thoughts, that she didn't know of his son and could take the stone without guilt.

But she did know, and she put her plan into place regardless. At the end of the week, they found themselves anxiously receiving the jeweler they had commissioned to replicate the stone. The slim-figured man with dainty fingers had carefully sketched the stone from Fergus' neck, never once asking why he would not remove it. Now, he pulled out a narrow black velvet cushion and pulled aside a layer of cloth to reveal the replica.

She and Fergus leaned close to the cushion, their breath held to determine if the expense of the remainder of Fergus' gold had been worthwhile. The green stone glittered in the candlelight, the simple gold chain delicate as a cobweb. Perfectly identical.

"It's glass, of course." The goldsmith shifted the cushion beneath the stone. The light caught at it and flashed in the heart of the fake gem as though it were made of fire within. He caught the delicate strand in the frame of his long fingers and held it aloft.

"It doesn't look like glass." Cassandra ducked her head and allowed the man to place it about her neck. The stone settled cool against her chest. But the true Heart of Scotland was warm, imbued with a life of its own.

"It looks bonny on ye, lass." Fergus lightly touched her face.

*The glass will warm when ye wear it.*

His words whispered in her mind, conveyed through the true stone. She nodded in agreement and tried to quell her doubt that the plan would work. It had seemed feasible before. But now with them being so very close to Edinburgh, so close to whatever awaited them there, she worried it wouldn't be enough.

If they failed, Fergus' son may die.

If she failed, Scotland could die.

Failure could not happen, and yet she had to face the truth of its possibility.

Fergus closed the door behind the departing goldsmith and turned to Cassandra. "Are ye ready?"

Her heart went wild in her chest. She had been born ready, for exactly this purpose. They had waited for this moment, being close enough to Edinburgh to get the stone. And now it was time. Doing it too soon would have the land repairing itself quickly, noticeably. She only hoped it was late enough that real damage had set in.

Fergus pulled the stone from his neck as Cassandra did likewise with the replica. His breath grunted out in a harsh exhale when the stone left its place against his chest. He gritted his teeth and held it to her with a trembling hand.

The blood raced through her veins and the whole of her world focused in on the dangling green gem, like a starving man before a feast, practically mad with ravenous need. She took the gold chain in her hand and vaguely had the sense he removed the duplicate from her. Her breath echoed loud in her own ears and her heartbeat thundered loudly.

Nay, it was not her heartbeat - it was that of Scotland beneath her.

She slipped the stone over her head and a surge flared through her. It expanded inside of her chest where it lay, burrowing deep and exploding outward in rays of energy so bright she thought surely it would extinguish her mortal life. She curled into it, embracing rather than fighting, and let the immensity of it absorb into her.

Strength fired through her, confidence, pure power. She surveyed the world and found it crackling with possibility.

"Incredible, aye?" Fergus asked with a smirk.

His hesitation removing it was understandable now that she had the force of the stone in her possession. It must have taken an amazing amount of will for him to pull it from his body.

"It did," he answered her thoughts grimly. "Though I can

scarcely hear yer mind without the clarity the stone afforded me."

She reached forward and took his hand in hers. She wanted him to experience the enormity of her gratitude for what he did with his sacrifice. The earth sang in joy, the beauty of its happiness rose into the air.

Pain edged into Cassandra's awareness and she realized it was not hers, but Fergus'. His hand. She squeezed it too tightly.

She gasped and released him, but he merely chuckled.

"Ye'll get used to yer talent soon." He massaged his hand. "'Tis fine."

He unclasped the shutters and let in the light of a new day. "The snow has ceased. It will take two days at most to get to Edinburgh from here with the ground still mired from the harsh weather." He leaned out and craned his head upward, squinting against the sun. "I only hope the weather isna so bonny it causes suspicion."

Cassandra joined him and gazed out at the bustling square below. Snow glittered against the brightness overhead and jagged blocks of ice had already begun to melt. It was certainly *not* the weather they had experienced without reprieve since Fergus first put on the stone. And yet Cassandra did not think she could bring herself to pull the stone from her chest as he had. Indeed, it would never leave her chest. Not when Scotland sang with such beautiful relief in her soul.

He turned to her. "We must go."

She nodded and gathered her things silently. Despite the completeness of her renewed strength and vigor from wearing the stone, she still harbored some hesitation that her plan would work. Her failure would bring about dire results, all of which would be revealed in two days' time.

∼

FERGUS TREAD heavily upon the ground with an exhaustible weight. It had been that way since he'd drawn the stone from his neck two days ago and given it to Cassandra.

Ever since, he had not seen with the same precision people's emotions. Their thoughts were muted, as though traveling beneath water rather than clear in his mind. He touched Cassandra whenever possible, drinking in the energy coursing through her veins in greedy sips every time their skin connected.

Edinburgh rose before them with its slanted streets and the massive castle atop the hill overlooking all the subjects below. It had been his home for the prior decade and yet it had never felt so foreign.

He wanted nothing more than to go within its bowels, claim the son he had never known and spirit him away from this place with its awful memories and painful past. Throughout the time of their journey, Fergus had sensed Cassandra's doubt at the plan, at her own survival.

Fergus had to concentrate especially hard, not just through his own softened abilities, but also through the column of energy surrounding her. Yet still, he could hear her thoughts: *she was afraid*. Not for herself, or her life, but of failure, and the lives that would be lost.

He clasped her slender hand in his to lead her through the crowded streets of Edinburgh. The power of the stone immediately shot to his palm and radiated out to the rest of his body.

Above, the skies were gray and snow had fallen intermittently through the day. He was glad for the sun having slipped behind the heavy clouds, for it gave the world a less sunlit appearance, one not indicative of the stone being in the Protector's care.

The king clearly had knowledge of the stone and the legend. Surely he would know the adverse effects of Fergus' wearing it.

Edinburgh Castle rose before them from its perch at the crest of the tall hill. They were almost there.

Excitement and uncertainty raced through his veins. Cassandra squeezed his hand and her thoughts merged with his own, warm with the recollection of the night before. They had stayed up far later than they ought to before battle. The night had been sweetly spent while they took their time cherishing one another, savoring what might never be again.

Even now, he wanted to draw her in his arms and press his lips to hers one final time. For neither knew the outcome ahead of them.

A flash of red hair showed in the crowd in front of them. Not an ordinary red, but brilliant, that shone even in the muted light of the overcast day. It caught his attention and Cassandra's hand tightened on his.

He'd only ever known one woman to possess such hair. Strange.

The crowd grew thicker when they pressed to the front of the gate. Peasants sought alms and people cried out their need to see the king to settle petty squabbles. The woman with red hair moved through the guards with ease and disappeared into a crowd of nobles within. A chill trickled down Fergus' spine. The likeness was eerie. Aye, that was it, what he was feeling. An eeriness.

He pushed his way to the guards with Cassandra behind him, his bulk clearing the crowd aside for her. The two guards closed the path before him despite his size, and met his gaze with steely resolution.

"I am Fergus the Undefeated," he said with all the authority imbued in such a name.

The guards' eyes widened and they immediately stood aside to let him pass. One of them turned and ran toward the castle, no doubt to inform the king. Cassandra's pulse raced against the heel of Fergus' hand and yet the churning anxiety she'd cast earlier settled to a surprising calm.

*She was ready.*

She nodded at him, as if to confirm he had heard her thoughts correctly. He nodded in return. For they would do this together, and they would be victorious. They had to be.

Fergus kept his hand clasped around hers though the thinned crowds within the castle did not warrant it. Together they were strong.

They were nearly to the throne room when the woman with red hair turned the corner in front of them, her back facing them. It had been ten years, a lifetime ago, but seeing her from that angle, Fergus knew without question who it was, however impossible it may be.

Or perhaps not. He could have easily been fed lies.

Regardless, he let go of Cassandra's hand in his determination to know, and closed the distance between himself and the red haired woman. She spun to face him, her green eyes wide with surprise, and confirmed his suspicions.

"Fergus," she whispered in awe.

He stared down at her as though he'd seen a ghost, for surely he had. "Allisandre."

## CHAPTER 12

Cassandra stood rooted in awkward shock. This woman with her flame red hair and luscious curves was Fergus' wife? His *dead* wife?

Quite alive, Allisandre put her hands to Fergus' face and pressed her full lips to his. Cassandra's stomach twisted. It was the very way she had bestowed her own affection to Fergus before. Had she been doing it the same as his wife all these weeks?

Fergus, for his part, stood rigidly in front of Allisandre. "They said ye died in childbirth."

"Clearly I have not." She gave a lovely little laugh and smoothed her hands down the front of her dress as though she were nervous. "They have kept me locked up, summoning me only now. They told me..." She touched her fingers to his lips with wonder. "They told me ye were dead."

Cassandra stared hard at Fergus and willed herself to hear his thoughts. Yet without touching him, she could not hear what he was thinking, not even with the stone. Nay, she was merely left miserable, standing by and wondering. The battle she had prepared to face was a welcome alternative to this.

"They have our son, Fergus." Allisandre drew in a shuddering breath. "They have Geordie."

Fergus flinched at that. The name. The one he had wondered for ten long years. Who was Cassandra to begrudge him this happiness, or worse, keep him from it?

"Do ye have it?" Allisandre put a hand to Fergus' chest, directly over the swell of his firm muscles.

Cassandra had loved to touch him there. She ought to look away, to break the pain of seeing their interaction, and yet found she could not.

"I have the stone," Fergus confirmed.

"Did you bring the Protector?" Allisandre turned and scanned the hallway. Her bright green eyes skimmed past Cassandra and searched the space behind her.

"Aye." Fergus indicated Cassandra who did her best to appear impassive despite the obvious snub.

"Her?" Allisandre's brows lifted with blatant disbelief. "She's a scrap of a thing, isn't she?"

Fergus' jaw clenched. For her part, Cassandra didn't know what to make of his reaction, and wished she didn't care.

Rather than dwell on it, she fixed her focus to the task at hand. After all, she was counting on being underestimated. Instead, she set her mind to the plan. She was there to save Fergus' son, and she was here to see her role as Protector met.

The stone lay against her skin, over her heart, rightfully strung about her neck and carefully hidden beneath the neckline of her wool dress.

The world was setting itself back into position with it in her care. It would not be undone, not even to prevent her own death.

Allisandre turned her back to Cassandra as though she were of little consequence. She reached for Fergus' hand, but he had stepped away from her, putting too much distance between them for her to touch him.

He did not move closer. Instead, he pushed open the massive double doors leading to the throne room.

Cassandra strode behind Fergus and Allisandre, and caught the distinctly sharp scent of magic in the air. Were it not for what she'd seen through Fergus' mind, she would never have been so poignantly aware of its redolence. But with the memory of his association, the knowledge of its presence sent an edge of warning rasping down her spine.

Why would Allisandre smell like magic?

She was so focused on the other woman, she did not realize Fergus had stopped in front of her, and clumsily bumped into the back of him. The image of Allisandre flickered in front of her, shifting from a beautiful young woman with sumptuous locks of red hair to an old woman, plump and gray with age.

Cassandra had stepped away from Fergus once she hit him, the mumble of apology immediate on her lips. But after the flash of an image, she moved forward once more, to touch him again and confirm what she had seen. A guard rushed forward and pulled her back from Fergus before she could touch him. The slam of the doors closing echoed in the greatness of the large, open room. They were trapped within.

She allowed the guard in black chain mail to drag her back, as though she did not possess the strength to fend him off. Let this man think he could easily subdue her. Let them all see and believe as much as well. It would be to her benefit.

It was not time for them to see their folly. At least, not yet.

"Enough," the man said gruffly. He shoved her to the side, putting her at Fergus' left, barely more than an arm's reach from him. Too far.

She stared hard at Fergus in an attempt to reclaim his attention. His gaze remained fixed ahead.

"This is the Protector?" A nasally voice echoed through the room and commanded Cassandra look forward.

On the throne was a slender man with dull yellow hair and shoulders bent forward as though the weight of the world rested upon his rounded back. He openly assessed her with glittering, greedy eyes.

"Remove her cloak and take her bags." He settled back against his throne as though bored. Guards in blackened chain mail came forward and plucked her bag from her grasp. The wet scent of magic clung to each of them.

Something important to keep forefront in her mind.

She unclasped her cloak and gave it to them before they could pull it from her body. It didn't matter. None of it did, for she had no use for anything but the stone, which lay tucked beneath the safety of her kirtle.

The king's gaze slid down Cassandra's body, rude with appreciation. Fergus tensed at her side.

Whether King Edgar noticed or not, he gave a wolfish grin and curled his fingers in a beckoning gesture aimed at Fergus while his eyes continued to feast on Cassandra. "Give me the stone."

Her heartbeat came faster. This was what she had spent the last several months building toward. The journey had stretched out to over two months with injury and weather, love and pain, and it had culminated to this moment.

Fergus obediently pulled off the necklace. The bit of green glass spun on the delicate gold chain and winked in the light from the rows of candles lining the cold chamber. The king nodded to Allisandre who took the replica and carried it to him before resuming her place at Fergus' right.

The king accepted the imposter stone and regarded where it lay cradled in his palm. The length of delicate gold chain draped from between his open fingers. Fergus' body jerked beside her a fraction of a second before the king tossed the fake to the ground and slammed his foot upon it. When he lifted his shoe, a million pieces of dust and shards glittered on the ground.

The weight of every eye in the room fell upon Cassandra and the warmth of the stone against her skin intensified, though mayhap it was merely her imagination, or possibly her nerves. She drew in a long, slow breath to steady herself.

This was what she had truly intended, the part of her plan she had blocked from Fergus. For he would never have agreed to it.

The day she had discovered his true plan to betray her, she knew she needed a way to get the stone from his possession. This had been the only way. In a perfect scenario, the king would have accepted the glass as the Heart of Scotland and she would have walked free with Fergus and his son. In a failed scenario, as Cassandra had feared would come to pass, and appeared to be doing so now, the king would not accept the counterfeit offering.

Most importantly, the stone was in her possession. Scotland was safe. And it would remain so.

Already the scent of magic pressed in on her, and she caught sight of the guards creeping closer through her periphery. Not that she would surrender.

Nay, she would fight.

If she were strong enough, she could somehow save Fergus' son, but the goal of saving Scotland was greater. The stone would not leave her throat, not until she had succeeded and walked from the chamber, or until she died. Either way, her role as Protector, her greater purpose in her short life, would be fulfilled.

But it was not her the guards seized. It was Allisandre. They held her between them and set a blade to her throat.

The king sat forward on his throne and the toe of his shoe

ground into the brittle glass beneath. "Give me the stone or she will die."

Fergus turned to Cassandra, his gaze pleading.

Cassandra lifted her head. "Nay."

The king's face colored. "Convince her."

"Please," Fergus hissed. "She has been a victim of this too. It isna right-"

"Nay," Cassandra repeated again, louder this time and with more defiance.

"Convince her or I will kill yer son," the king bellowed.

Fergus' pleading gaze melted to desperation, the pain in his eyes visceral enough to plunge into the most tender place in her heart. "Cassandra," he said in a strained voice.

She turned her face away from him, unable to witness his agony as she gave her final answer. "Nay."

∼

FERGUS STARED at Cassandra in disbelief. She had condemned his son to death. Geordie. The lad he had never met, never held in his arms. The boy whose name he had only just learned minutes before.

Cassandra's face remained fixed toward the king, as if she could not bear to look at him. Indeed, how could she with what she had just done?

"Dinna do this." Fergus stepped toward her and grabbed her arm. The energy of the stone crackled through her and raced into his body. The thoughts and emotions of others whirled around him with Cassandra's thoughts rising above them all.

*Look at her.*

He knew who Cassandra meant. He put his attention to his wife, the woman he had once loved for her beauty and the fresh smell of rain about her. The woman he realized he no longer felt anything for.

Not that it meant she ought to die.

Allisandre struggled against her captors. Even in her terror, her face remained youthful and supple, her skin without the slightest wrinkle. She looked exactly as she had the day he'd met her twelve years ago. Beautiful. Perfect.

*Truly look at her.*

Fergus fixed his gaze harder. Her image flickered, briefly like the wavering heat of a flame. The memory of her smell locked in his brain, the delicate scent flooded with the horrors of his nightmare. It wasn't an essence of something fresh upon her all those years - it was magic.

*Beyond her block.*

Aye, Allisandre's secrets. The ones she insisted all women had, her smile cold with warning when she'd said it. It had worked when he was young and infatuated, his experience untried and without the aid of the stone. He drew deep from the stone and glared at the woman struggling against her captors.

Except she was no longer there. Gone was the woman of unnatural timeless beauty and in her place was an old woman with frizzing gray hair and breasts that sagged against her soft belly.

He staggered back, as did the others, all horrified by her dropped mask.

"Do not touch her," Allisandre shrieked. Her hand shot up and Fergus flew into the air, torn from Cassandra's grasp.

"Ye love me, remember?" She grinned at him with yellowed teeth.

Fergus hung aloft only a second more before Allisandre whipped her hand to the right and sent him soaring across the room. His body crashed hard into the stone wall. His chain mail absorbed none of the impact and instead shoved it painfully against his body. The force holding him slipped away and he dropped several feet to the floor below. Agony exploded at his left side and he curled around it, hissing out his discomfort.

"Allisandre," he ground out.

Cassandra raced toward Allisandre at an unnaturally fast pace, but Allisandre cupped her palms toward Cassandra and she stopped in place, struggling against an unseen force. Magic was thick in the air, cloying where it lodged in the back of Fergus' throat.

A hearty laugh came from the front of the room. The king clapped his hand upon his thigh, the way he might do for a troubadour's performance. "Ye were right, Lachina. He dinna ever suspect ye."

The old woman smirked at the king. "He canna track people who dinna exist."

Fergus' mind reeled. The thoughts and emotions of the room were murky to him, a blur throbbing in time with the ache in his skull. What in God's teeth were they talking about?

The king grinned, his eyes lit with victory. "Guards, collect the girl and bring her to me. She has something I want."

Fergus' awareness latched to the king's and saw exactly what the king wished to do with Cassandra. His muscles flared with white hot heat and he roared in protest. He moved forward three steps. Four. Five, pushing through the magic binding him.

Allisandre put up another hand and stayed him. Fergus growled and fought, even while his brain reeled. Not Allisandre. Lachina?

"Who are ye?" he demanded. "What happened to Allisandre?"

A handful of men in black chain mail surrounded Cassandra and locked their hands over her slender arms. One soldier stood behind her, his elbow crooked under her chin at her throat.

The witch rolled her eyes at Fergus. "There never was an

Allisandre, ye fool. It was how we were able to trick ye into believing she was dead. If she were a real person, dinna ye think ye'd have felt her?"

He shook his head, refusing to believe what Lachina said. After all, he had held Allisandre in his arms, he had kissed her, and he had stared into those brilliant green eyes. A shiver rattled through him. The memory surfaced, real and true - the unnaturally green eyes and the intensity of her stare, as though she meant to devour him. Or control him.

Nausea rolled through his stomach. All of it had been a lie. His life had been a lie.

The men pushed Cassandra to the dais where the king drummed his fingers over the arm of the throne with dramatic impatience. Fergus fought harder against the unseen wall holding him back, but it did not yield.

He had been lied to, deceived. A horrifying thought shot through him, as sharp and painful as a marksman's arrow. Lachina was too old to bear a child.

His heart slammed against his ribs. "What of my son?" he asked in a voice he could not keep from trembling. "What of Geordie?"

The king glanced to the witch with the mirth of those sharing a cruel joke. Together they gave a malicious bark of laughter.

His stomach slid lower.

Nay.

"Dinna be so foolish." Lachina shook her head, her eyes sparkling. She slid another look to the king, but he was occupied with Cassandra who stood a foot away.

"Did ye no' hear what I told ye before?" Lachina's bushy gray brows crinkled her forehead upward. "Ye canna track people who dinna exist."

Fergus gritted his teeth and a knot of tension tightened at the back of his throat. "What do ye mean?"

"Ye know what I mean," she snarled.

The king reached for Cassandra, his slender white hand stretching toward her neck.

"Say it," Fergus demanded. The vehemence of his voice echoed off the cold stone and shot back at him.

"Did ye ever once feel the lad in yer mind?" the witch countered.

"Say it," Fergus roared. His vision dotted with white and his palms tingled.

"Ye daft lout." The witch spat upon the ground. "Yer son dinna ever exist anymore than yer wife did."

Fergus ceased fighting the magic and staggered back against the wall. That was it. The entire life Fergus had sacrificed for, what he had led Cassandra to her death for and abandoned his mother to a lonely estate for, all of it had been for naught.

He balled his hands into fists at his side and howled with the force of a demon. He had lost everything.

## CHAPTER 13

Cassandra had bided her time, and guarded her talents until now. The king had his suspicions about her, she'd seen as much in his thoughts when Fergus had touched her arm.

King Edgar thought her too slight, too insignificant to be a threat - even with the stone's power behind her. He had underestimated her. They all had.

Exactly as she had planned.

Fergus' agonized cry reverberated through her and left her heart trembling with sorrow for his loss. There was no son to rescue. There was nothing more to save, except Scotland.

Cassandra gripped the guard's arm locked over her throat to hold the man against her back, and bent over while drawing him forward. The man fought against the momentum with a speed only an enchantment could afford him. But her action had been too sudden, too unexpected. He flew over her head and collided with the king.

The men surrounding her glided forward, so quickly she almost didn't have time to stop them. She drew all the force of her strength, unrestrained for the first time in her life, and enhanced with the force of the stone. Her fist connected with the first one and arced onward, to the second, the third, the fourth, and fifth. The men were launched into the air and landed nearly ten feet away from her. Three rose, two did not.

In fact, two were no longer there.

Cassandra crouched to the ground and splayed her open hands over the stonework there. She pushed her energy out and let it connect with the earth. The building groaned and dust sifted from the rafters. The flagstones underfoot trembled, a low vibration first before growing to a rattle. An unseen force wrapped around her. Squeezing, squeezing, squeezing, like a giant fist. The air crackled.

Magic.

She gritted her teeth and shot upward, breaking through the invisible hold. She put her hand to the floor and it rumbled violently. Deep fissures cut into the ground and jagged outward like the rays of a sun.

Something dark flew at her, but she deflected the advance of a soldier with the shift of her forearm. Another came at her so quickly, she was forced to lift her other arm. When the third came at her, she had no more arms. The man struck her in the face full force. She rocked backward and the grip of magic closed around her once more.

"Kill her," the king snarled in the distance. "But get that damn necklace first."

Cassandra flexed her body with the exertion of energy and ripped through the shell of magic. This time she focused her attention on the witch. Cassandra wrenched a clawed hand upward. Green vines snaked from the cracked floor and slithered toward Lachina. The woman backed up, but there were more coming from behind.

Lachina swept her palm outward, fighting the stone's strength with magic. Some vines shrank back, but still others crept forward. Fergus staggered as the force keeping him held fell away, and ran toward Cassandra.

She vaguely heard his hoarse cry call her name, but she could not let her attention fix on him. Not when she had a very potent witch to contend with. A witch who was losing the battle.

A soldier cracked his fist against Cassandra's head. She rocked, briefly acknowledging the pain of the strike. Sweat beaded on her brow as she fought the resistance from the witch and kept the vines racing onward. They had spiraled up the woman's red skirt and twisted about her waist.

Another guard darted at Cassandra and swept his leg against the back of her knees while yet another still threw a solid kick directly into the center of her chest. Pain exploded at her breastbone and stole the breath from her lungs.

Her connection to the earth faltered for a brief moment and the vines shrank back.

Yet another man moved behind her in a blur of motion. He clutched her shoulders and jerked her backward. Cassandra lost her footing and connected with the hard ground.

In that brief moment, before she could suck in a deep inhalation to clear her mind, the soldiers were on her. Their black chain mail moved about with a speed that made them no more possible to capture than wisps of smoke. Brutal hands turned her over and jerked her arms back. She snatched her limbs back and leapt deftly to her feet.

She would not go down so easily.

The breath wheezed from her chest, each one as painful as though she drew in fire instead of air. Blood dotted the floor at her feet and a swirling in her head told her the strike to her temple had done some damage.

The stone may have imbued her with strength, but it did not increase the durability of her mortal body. Even with the soldiers charging at her, the witch was the greatest threat.

Cassandra swept her hand and drew all the breathable air toward her in a rush. The men coughed and choked, their magic as unprepared for the inability to breathe as her ability had been against protecting her from strikes.

Cassandra shoved her hands toward Lachina who wrestled with the vines still locked over her shins. The stone burned against Cassandra's chest, but she ignored it and let all of herself be consumed with its strength. It blazed through her like the light of the stars and the moon and the sun all at once. White flooded her vision and streaked from her fingertips.

Her throat rasped with a scream and the vines redoubled their effort until they had wrapped the witch completely. They coiled over her shoulders, her throat, her face, the top of her head, and then she was nothing more than a writhing mass of rapacious vines pulsing and flexing around her.

The surge calmed and pulled with it the unnatural strength. Cassandra staggered back and gasped in a burning breath. The air whooshed back into the room.

"Dinna stop, ye fools." The king's impatience pitched into something of a shriek. "I want that bloody stone now."

A soldier flew at her, but not in attack. He skidded over the floor before coming to a stop inches from her feet and fading. Another figure rushed in front of her, the movements slower, more natural. Fergus. He was at her side. His dark eyes met hers and he held out his left hand, his less dominant one when fighting.

They always were stronger together.

Cassandra placed her palm in his and the energy between them surged anew.

Fergus hadn't realized how badly Cassandra had been wounded. Not until he touched her and was slammed by the wave of pain rolling toward him. Still, he kept his alarm guarded from her awareness. Though her body was badly battered, and her energy flagging, he sensed in her a determination that would not be stopped. Fear would only minimize her skills.

Damn Lachina for having kept him captive by her magic, away from the fighting. It had been torture watching her take hits he could have prevented. The fight had been unfair – until now.

He shared his ability with Cassandra, allowing her to see the intended movements of their foes at a speed she could match. The breath rasped from her mouth, but her strikes were sure and lethal. With hands clasped tight, the two of them fought side-by-side, talents and efforts combined.

The soldiers had lost the advantage of magic. One by one they fell beneath the power and the skill afforded to Cassandra and Fergus by the stone. Every now and then, a soldier might get in a punch or a kick, for it was impossible to block so many coming at once.

Cassandra tensed at his side.

*The witch is connected to them.*

Fergus flicked a glance at Cassandra. He'd thought Lachina dead beneath the vines.

Cassandra punched a man in the throat. Through her, Fergus felt the crunch of the soldier's windpipe against her knuckles as he lurched back and disappeared.

*If she is dead, they will be gone.*

Fergus nodded at Cassandra's thoughts, unspoken and yet fully understood between them. She would concentrate on her skills while he defended them both. Cassandra closed her eyes, fully trusting in his capability. He sensed the hum of energy rising in her and filling her palm, which she closed into a fist. The vines acted on her will and squeezed.

The guard in front of Fergus flickered in and out, like a sputtering candle. Lachina's control was fading with her life.

"Harder," Fergus demanded. He gripped Cassandra's free hand and fought with his right hand, his blade cutting down man after man, bastards in blackened chain, a bloody endless supply of them.

The crowd of soldiers pressed forward with a renewed effort, a desperate effort, jabbing with fists and blades. With the benefit of the stone, every one of their intended actions were visible to Fergus, and easily blocked. It was a defense he didn't have the ability to wield ten years earlier when he was not strong enough.

Blood welled between Cassandra's fingers and dripped from her fist. She did not register the pain he felt from her, but instead tightened her fist even more. The soldiers began to fade, their movements growing slower, more clumsy.

And then one ran forward from the crowd, crisply outlined where the others blurred, his movements faster than even the stone could register. A knife glinted. Too fast. Too fast.

It punched forward, not at Fergus, but at Cassandra, and lodged in her side.

Her head fell back and a soft cry escaped her lips. All at once the soldiers faded from view and Cassandra drooped. Fergus caught her with his free arm and carefully lowered her to the ground. The breath hissed in her chest and blood bubbled at the corner of her mouth. He'd seen this type of injury before. One he knew to be fatal. Pain filled his chest, not only from the burning of the difficult breathing she suffered from, but also from the ache in his own heart.

He couldn't lose her. Not when he'd lost so much that day. She released his hand, severing their connection, and gripped the hilt jutting from her side, her skin white against the polished onyx. "The king," she hissed.

"Nay," he cried. But even as he spoke, he knew he could not stop her from pulling the blade from her body. The dagger loosened with a wet sucking sound followed by a choked exhale. Blood dotted her lips.

She shoved the dagger to him, still glistening red. "The... king..." she wheezed between the words with pained breath.

As she spoke, a shuffle met Fergus' awareness. The distinct sound of someone trying carefully and discreetly to flee. Fergus honed his attention on the slender man, and narrowed his eyes like a predator ready to catch its prey.

The king's movements fanned out long before he took them, easily apparent after the magically imbued guards, giving Fergus enough time to properly aim his blade. He touched Cassandra's hand, now freed of the dagger and drew from the waning power of the stone to send the dagger launching toward the king with all the force their combined strength could possess.

The weapon punched into the king's chest with such force, it sent him careening backward into the far wall where he slunk like a discarded poppet. He did not rise. Hell, he didn't even struggle, the bastard. So damn easy to kill without his army of magic at his back.

Cassandra choked and the hand under Fergus' flinched. He snapped his attention to her as her body relaxed, relinquishing her mortal struggle. His heart sucked up into his throat.

"Cassandra," he said tightly. He shook his head, unable to say more against the tension in his throat.

Her bloody fist loosened, her fingers unfurling to reveal where her fingernails had scored deep enough into her palms that the white tendons beneath showed. Immediately the vines gripping Lachina uncoiled and fell limp. The witch was nowhere in sight, the same as the men she controlled.

Fergus wrapped his hand against Cassandra's, but felt nothing. No force of the stone, no wild connection of energy. No pulse.

Heat prickled at his eyelids. He had failed her. It was as it had been ten years before, but this time with someone real. Someone he…

Someone he loved.

She wavered, the same as the soldiers had when Lachina was dying. The stone disappeared for a moment before reappearing faintly, more like a skein of sunlight than a physical form. Cassandra was dying.

## CHAPTER 14

Fergus could not lose Cassandra. He squeezed her hand in search for the stone's connection to flare between them, a sensation he had too often taken for granted.

Nothing happened.

He pulled deep from the anguish inside him and a cry escaped him, raw and savage. His voice echoed around him again and again and again through the vast stone chamber. A mockery of his pain, of his loss. Because he could not lose her. He would rather die than have her taken from the earth.

He didn't know why he did it, but he took her clasped hand and set it over his heart. "Take my life," he said, muttering as though in prayer. "And give it to her who is worthy."

Her fingers fell limp over his own and her form flickered.

"Take it," he cried.

A bone-searing pain bolted through him, as though his soul were being sucked from his body. He jolted forward with the force of it. It pulled at him, suckling the life from his body and funneling it into Cassandra through their joined hands.

"Stop." Her voice was weak, but it was the most beautiful sound in all the world.

"Live, Cassandra," he said through gritted teeth. "Live."

"Not without you." She jerked her hand from his.

Energy sparked between them with streaks of magic stretching between their fingers like ribbons of lightning. She gasped for breath and then gave a soft laugh. "You saved me, Fergus."

He shook his head. "Nay, lass. It's ye who saved me."

She ran a weak hand through his hair. "You were killing yourself."

"I was giving ye life." He stared down at her, unable to take his gaze from the soft curls of dark hair falling about her fair face. Her lips were as lush and red as they'd ever been, her pale blue eyes bright with unshed tears. "I love ye, Cassandra."

She blinked, but a tear escaped the corner of her eye. "And I you, Fergus. I think I have since the day I met you."

"And I ye." He smiled to himself at the memory. "Since the first time I saw ye in the apple orchard in a vision." He eyed the blood at the side of her gown where it stood bright against the pale lavender. "We must leave from here. Can ye walk?"

She nodded, but still winced as she rose. Her gaze immediately fell on the king and she lifted her beautiful gaze to Fergus in question. "We are free?"

He smiled, the first carefree smile he could remember in far too long. "Aye," he answered. "We are free."

"But at what cost?" she fingered his hair.

He frowned with confusion.

"You have a strip of white that was not there before. I worry..." She pursed her lips. "I worry what you have sacrificed in saving me."

"I would have sacrificed it all," he vowed.

She smiled sadly. "I know."

She closed her eyes briefly and waved a hand. The vines sucked deep into the cracks within the floor and the fissures sealed upon themselves. Save the dead king crumpled in the corner, it was as though none of it had ever happened.

Cassandra's brow furrowed and a wild wind billowed outside, rattling doors and windows. Thunder shuddered overhead and the roar of a sleeting rainstorm immediately followed.

She opened her eyes and smiled. "A little chaos to aid in our escape while you clear the memories of those who saw us."

He shook his head, but she nodded. "You can. I saw it." She linked her fingers with his. "Or rather we can together."

They clasped hands and breathed as one. They expanded their minds in unison, threading it through the whole of Edinburgh, locating and plucking their images from the minds of all who saw them until they never existed in the memory of the people.

"What of him?" Cassandra asked when they were done, indicating the king with her mind.

"There is much family strife." Fergus stared at the limp form of the king who had threatened him for the whole of a decade. "Let them think it was his uncle who killed him."

She nodded and allowed Fergus to offer her the support of his body as he led her to a back room where he knew there to be an unseen exit. Her movements were slow, her breathing labored. While her presence no longer flickered with the threat of death, she was still not recovered.

"I'm well enough," she argued and then stumbled.

He caught her before she fell. His hand had splayed over her slender stomach by accident. A heartbeat thundered against his palm. He jerked his hand back in wonder.

Cassandra's eyes went wide, having experienced the same realization as he. Her skin held a sickly pallor and her brow glistened with an unhealthy sheen. "Fergus..." She put her hand to her flat stomach that would not remain so for long.

He nodded, hearing her thoughts before she could get them through the emotion clogging her words.

"I do have a son." He stroked her face. "And a wife." He grinned. "If ye'll have me."

Tears shone bright in Cassandra's eyes. "Nothing would bring me greater joy."

"Nor I," he said. "Save seeing ye safe." He hefted her feet from beneath her and cradled her to his chest as though she weighed nothing, for surely to Fergus the Undefeated she did not.

She relaxed into the embrace of his arms, the glow of contentment spreading between them both from their own joy and through the elation of the other. "I happen to be acquainted with one of the best healers in all of Scotland," she said with a smile.

Fergus grinned. "Then mayhap we should go see her."

Cassandra nodded. "Indeed we should."

They slipped discreetly and unseen from Edinburgh, and ventured to Inverness on sunlit paths until they were once more met with happiness and love and the quiet joy of Blair.

# EPILOGUE
JUNE 1109

Giggles erupted from the other side of the garden wall. Cassandra turned to Blair and the two of them shared a smile.

"I believe I hear the sound of a wee lad on his way to see his Ma." Blair lifted the basket of freshly snipped herbs to her side.

"And his Grandmama," Cassandra said with a wink.

"Ach, aye, from time to time he's glad to see me as well." Blair's eyes sparkled as she said it.

Though it was hardly from 'time to time' for little Niven when it came to his eldmother. Fergus rounded the corner to the garden with the toddler on his back. The boy squealed with delight and put his dimpled hands over Fergus' eyes in his excitement.

"I canna see," Fergus cried with great theatrics, which only served to send Niven into greater fits of giggles.

Fergus plucked the boy from his shoulders with both hands and gently set him upon the ground. Niven toddled over the uneven ground to Cassandra and Blair with his clumsy gait, and caught his fists into the skirts of both. "Are you tired, my little love?" Cassandra asked, hefting his scant weight into her arms.

He rubbed at his eyes and shook his head. His lower lip thrust outward in a miserable pout and he met her gaze with the dark, soulful stare he'd inherited from his father. He shifted in Cassandra's arms and the weight of his head settled against the crook of her neck. The gentle blend of rosemary and lavender and little boy sweat rose from his silky dark hair.

Cassandra drew a deep breath of her son and her heart swelled with all the joy he brought to her life. She brushed her lips over his silky hair in a cherished kiss. He pushed her away moodily.

"Are ye sure ye're no' tired?" Blair walked her fingers up Niven's soft arm to the crook of his delicate neck.

He scrunched his shoulder to his ear and shoved at her.

"Not in need of a nap, indeed," Cassandra said slyly.

Blair laughed in her good-natured way. "I had a lad once who was far more a beast than my wee little Niven. Have ye heard that story?"

Niven shifted his head under Cassandra's chin to regard his eldmother. Fergus met Cassandra's eye and together they grinned, already knowing where this was going.

Niven shook his head against Cassandra's neck.

"Ach, it's a fine story." Blair held out her hands and the little boy pulled away from his mother with arms outstretched toward his eldmother.

"I loved the demons out of him." She pulled him into her arms and winked at Cassandra, knowing there was a need for privacy between her and Fergus. Especially this day of all days.

"I hugged it out of him." Blair strode away with the boy in her arms and squeezed him a playfully large, rocking embrace. "I kissed it out of him." The pucker of a dozen kisses led them from the garden to where they could no longer be heard.

Fergus regarded Cassandra from the corner of his eye. "Ye have something to tell me." He concentrated a moment longer.

"And ye're blocking it from me." He untucked Niven's small wooden sword from his arm and propped it against the backside of the bench. The pretend weapon had been a gift from Phillip on his last visit to see them. He'd brought gifts for them all, including apples from the orchard, and news of home.

In truth the only thing that had interested Cassandra were the bits involving Phillip and the details of brave things he'd done - as was told in a boisterous tone with many different character's voices and much drama.

"Maybe you should learn not to read a woman's thoughts." Cassandra gave Fergus a coy smile and settled onto the stone bench beneath the shade of an apple tree.

Fergus had planted it when they'd arrived back in Inverness with Blair. And when Cassandra was fully healed, she had pressed upon the earth to help make it grow. In the summer, its shade was the coolest and in the summer and early fall, its apples were the sweetest.

Fergus took her face in his hands. His touch blazed through her veins like fire. Still. After over two years and a child born, each touch was as intense as their first.

"You cannot get through my defenses so easily, Fergus the Undefeated," she chided.

He nuzzled his lips to hers and teased her mouth apart for his tongue to sweep against hers.

"I think you cheat," she murmured.

He leaned back and grinned. "So I do. And so I will until ye tell me."

She took his hand and put it to her lower stomach where she sensed he could discern the healthy, steady thrum of another small heartbeat. Another child.

"A girl," he breathed. "Ye're no' happy."

Cassandra shook her head in protest and put her hand over

his. "I do not want our youngest daughter to go through life as I did, beneath the burden of obligation."

Fergus nodded. "I know what ye intend to do. But are ye no' sure it will be a curse upon our bloodline?"

Cassandra smiled at her husband and all the warmth of her love for him glowed through her. "I assure you, it will not."

She closed her eyes and, with the power drawn through both of them and the stone, she drew from the earth a promise that no one would remember the skills of a youngest daughter when she died, so the future generations would not be birthed into a life of expectation.

Her stomach grew warm and Fergus settled his hand over her more securely, as though he meant to protect her.

"She will have a good life," Cassandra reassured her husband.

"The way we do." He put his palm to her cheek once more and she flushed beneath the tenderness of his affection.

"Aye," she whispered. "She will be happy and she will be loved."

"And truly, there's no' anything else to need in life." With that, he kissed her sweetly and soundly, with the promise of so much more to come.

# ALSO BY MADELINE MARTIN

**The Borderland Ladies**

Ena's Surrender

Marin's Promise

Anice's Bargain

Ella's Desire

Catriona's Secret

Leila's Legacy

**The Borderland Rebels**

The Highlander's Lady Knight

Faye's Sacrifice

Kinsey's Defiance

Clara's Vow

Drake's Honor

**Highland Passions**

A Ghostly Tale of Forbidden Love

The Madam's Highlander

Her Highland Destiny

The Highlander's Untamed Lady

**Matchmaker of Mayfair**

Discovering the Duke

Unmasking the Earl

Mesmerizing the Marquis

Earl of Benton

Earl of Oakhurst

Earl of Kendal

**Heart of the Highlands**

Deception of a Highlander

Possession of a Highlander

Enchantment of a Highlander

**Standalones**

The Highlander's Challenge - N W M S

Her Highland Beast - N W M S (fairytale twist retelling - Beauty and the Beast/Princess and the Pea with Scottish folklore)

# ABOUT THE AUTHOR

Madeline Martin is a *New York Times, USA Today,* and International Bestselling author of historical fiction and historical romance with books that have been translated into over twenty different languages.

She lives in sunny Florida with her two daughters (known collectively as the minions), two incredibly spoiled cats and a man so wonderful he's been dubbed Mr. Awesome. She is a die-hard history lover who will happily lose herself in research any day. When she's not writing, researching or 'moming', you can find her spending time with her family at Disney or sneaking a couple spoonfuls of Nutella while laughing over cat videos. She also loves research and travel, attributing her fascination with history to having spent most of her childhood as an Army brat in Germany.

Check out her website for book club visits, reader guides for her historical fiction, upcoming events, book news and more: https://madelinemartin.com

Made in the USA
Columbia, SC
17 April 2023